Blow for Blow

Red's knuckles cracked against Clint's jaw and sent him sidestepping away from the saloon's front door. As he stepped forward, Red shook out the pain in his hand while grinning like he'd just won a prize.

"Maybe you should go back to wherever you came from," Red grunted.

Playing on the confidence in Red's voice, Clint kept his head down and leaned against the saloon. Once Red had strutted close enough, Clint balled up his own fist and sent it Red's way. His punch didn't make as much noise as Red's, but it drove far enough into the man's gut that he doubled over.

Red coughed and gritted his teeth. "That's the last mistake you're gonna make," he said, and he rushed toward Clint with both arms held open . . .

THE GUNSMITH

313

WILDFIRE

J. R. ROBERTS

JOVE BOOKS, NEW YORK

THE BERKLEY PUBLISHING GROUP
Published by the Penguin Group
Penguin Group (USA) Inc.
375 Hudson Street, New York, New York 10014, USA

Penguin Group (Canada), 90 Eglinton Avenue East, Suite 700, Toronto, Ontario M4P 2Y3, Canada
(a division of Pearson Penguin Canada Inc.)
Penguin Books Ltd., 80 Strand, London WC2R 0RL, England
Penguin Group Ireland, 25 St. Stephen's Green, Dublin 2, Ireland (a division of Penguin Books Ltd.)
Penguin Group (Australia), 250 Camberwell Road, Camberwell, Victoria 3124, Australia
(a division of Pearson Australia Group Pty. Ltd.)
Penguin Books India Pvt. Ltd., 11 Community Centre, Panchsheel Park, New Delhi—110 017, India
Penguin Group (NZ), 67 Apollo Drive, Rosedale, North Shore 0632 New Zealand
(a division of Pearson New Zealand Ltd.)
Penguin Books (South Africa) (Pty.) Ltd., 24 Sturdee Avenue, Rosebank, Johannesburg 2196,
South Africa

Penguin Books Ltd., Registered Offices: 80 Strand, London WC2R 0RL, England

This is a work of fiction. Names, characters, places, and incidents either are the product of the author's imagination or are used fictitiously, and any resemblance to actual persons, living or dead, business establishments, events, or locales is entirely coincidental.

WILDFIRE

A Jove Book / published by arrangement with the author

PRINTING HISTORY
Jove edition / January 2008

ISBN: 978-0-515-14398-0

JOVE®
Jove Books are published by The Berkley Publishing Group,
a division of Penguin Group (USA) Inc.,
375 Hudson Street, New York, New York 10014.
JOVE is a registered trademark of Penguin Group (USA) Inc.
The "J" design is a trademark belonging to Penguin Group (USA) Inc.

PRINTED IN THE UNITED STATES OF AMERICA

10 9 8 7 6 5 4 3 2 1

ONE

As he watched the shed burn, a tear came to his eye. The flames licked the walls and stretched upward as the smoke billowed out and drifted along the wind.

The longer he watched, the more his boots seemed to take root in the ground beneath him. He simply couldn't take his eyes from the spectacle of the orange and red flickering that resembled glowing water more than anything else.

Once the screams started, he knew he'd surely found his calling.

His eyes darted to both sides so he could quickly take a look around. Mostly, he was concerned about someone else coming along and trying to put out the fire or get to the folks that were trapped inside the burning shed.

But nobody was coming.

Once that became clear, the man crossed his arms and watched the shed burn.

The screams were getting louder now.

He guessed the flames had spread more inside the shed rather than just burning the outside of the walls. Closing his eyes to take in the voices instead of the flames, he listened to the cries and picked out the different ones the way some children might skip through a field and pick out just the flowers they wanted.

First, the cries had been frantic pleas. These had annoyed the man almost enough to put an end to them right then and there. Those two folks inside the shed had begged and whined to be set free. Once the man took the time to walk back inside, the pleas had turned to questions and more begging.

"Why me?"

"Why me?"

"Why are you doing this?"

Selfish little bastards. Why not them?

Thinking back to that, the man decided he wouldn't bother going back to check on the next ones he caught. Those first bunch of whines had been like an old rake being dragged against a sheet of rusty tin. The next time he got ahold of someone, he vowed not to go back when they begged. Otherwise, he might not get to hear the next set of screams before he put an end to their whining himself.

The next bunch of screams were better.

Those sounds had been full of hopelessness and fear. There wasn't any more begging. It was all sobbing and wailing. The man liked the sound of that quite a lot.

But now that the flames were just starting to lose some of their brightness and the smoke was really pouring out of the shack, the screams had reached a whole other plateau. They were filled with stark panic and raw terror.

The fire must really be getting to them now. It might have caught onto the bit of kerosene that the man had dripped on the backs of their chairs as a lark. Whatever the cause, the screams were piercing and went on for so long that the folks inside no longer seemed to need to draw a breath.

More than anything, the man wanted to take a peek inside the shed and get a look at what was happening there. In fact, the more he thought about it, the harder it was to keep himself from rushing through the crooked remains of the door frame.

Cocking his head a bit to one side, the man studied the door and saw that there was more smoke than flame in the opening. Perhaps the wood had burned up enough for him to step through without getting hurt too badly. He knew he could stand some pain. If it meant getting a look at those faces as they screamed, he could stand a whole lot of pain.

The screams were fading now, so there probably wasn't much time left before they were gone.

He took one step forward.

Then another.

Even though the heat was getting under his skin and the smoke was scratching down the back of his throat, he kept stepping toward the shed. Finally, the man reached out to push open a door that had already cracked and fallen down. When some of the flames reached out to blacken the tips of his fingers, he smiled.

"What are you doing? Get away from there!"

The man didn't always listen to the voice, but this time was different. This time, the voice shook him awake just in time to feel the heat that was about to swallow him up. When he tried to pull in a breath, it snagged and got him coughing in fits.

The screaming was almost gone now, so the man took a few steps back and listened to it.

When there was no more screaming, he listened to the flames eat up the rest of the shed.

TWO

The fire was long dead.

A few wisps of smoke drifted up from the depths of the wooden pile, but most of the smoke hung in a cloud over the spot where the fire had been. It put a grayness into the air and was stirred up by the morning breeze, like soup being pushed around by a spoon.

Clint lay on the ground next to the remains of his campfire and took a deep breath. The previous night's dinner hadn't been the best, but it had stuck to his bones well enough to give him a good night's sleep. Now that he was just starting to wake up, he decided to stretch out for a bit longer and savor the smells of early morning.

With his ear against the ground, he was able to hear the approaching horses well before he could have seen them. The rumbling was faint, but followed a distinctive rhythm. He knew of some Indians who claimed to be able to know the breed and size of a horse by hearing its steps. All Clint could tell was that there were a few horses out there and they were headed his way.

Unfortunately, that was enough to put an end to his hours of sleep.

Clint reached under his bedroll for the modified Colt that had been kept there within his reach while he slept. The pistol was in his hand before his feet were under him. Before he'd worked the kinks out of his neck, Clint had also found his gun belt and buckled it around his waist.

Possibly sensing Clint's uneasiness, the black Darley Arabian stallion tied off nearby shifted on its feet.

As he walked toward the sound of the approaching horses, Clint patted the stallion's nose and whispered, "It's all right, boy. Just keep quiet, now."

Although Eclipse had been with him for a good long while, Clint didn't seriously think the stallion could understand every word that was said to him. Then again, when Eclipse stopped shifting and fell silent, Clint wondered if he might have to rethink that assumption.

"Do you hear those horses coming?" Clint asked.

Eclipse stared straight ahead, eyeing a particularly thick patch of tall grass nearby.

Chuckling to himself, Clint pulled on his boots and buttoned his shirt. If the horses were coming closer, he figured it couldn't hurt to look a bit more presentable.

A minute or so later, he could hear the rumble of hooves without needing to put his ear to the ground. Now that he had a definite direction picked out, Clint dug out his spyglass and pointed it that way.

The sun was already bright and seemed even more so when reflected off the sands of New Mexico. Clint wasn't foolish enough to ride straight into the desert without good cause, but he was close enough to feel the ground favoring more rock than soil beneath him. There was also enough sand to be kicked up by anything bigger than a coyote.

Clint had no trouble spotting the dust cloud left behind by the horses. Thanks to the early morning sun, it was just as easy to pick out the horses and riders responsible for that cloud.

Nearby, Eclipse let out a few snuffling grunts and shifted some more.

"Hold on, boy," Clint muttered. "I'll untie you in a second."

"Don't bother with that," the stranger behind Clint replied. "You won't be going anywhere."

Clint's first reflex was to straighten up and turn around.

He got the first part of that accomplished and was stopped when the back of his head knocked against the barrel of a drawn pistol. Right about then, Clint found himself wishing he could have understood what Eclipse was trying to say a few seconds earlier.

"If you're looking to rob me," Clint said, "you'll be disappointed. I'm not carrying much of anything."

There was no reply.

"No?" Clint asked. "Then maybe you'd like some coffee. I was just about to brew some up."

Still nothing.

Clint took a cautious half step forward. The moment he moved, he could feel the man tensing behind him. Even so, Clint managed to get an inch or so of space between his head and the man's gun.

"If you're out to steal my horse," Clint said before turning completely around and dropping to one knee, "you're in for a fight."

The man who'd snuck up on Clint was a big fellow with broad shoulders and a mustache that drooped down past his chin. His eyes were squinting even though the sun was more or less at his back. Although his chest and stomach were thick, it was plain to see that it wasn't from too many meals.

Despite the natural harshness in the man's features, he blinked in surprise at how quickly Clint had turned around. Not only was Clint's head out of the man's immediate line of fire, but his hand had made it down to his holster and back up again before the bigger man could do a damn thing about it.

"All right," Clint said as he held his Colt at hip level and aimed up at the bigger man, "now we can talk. Who are you?"

"The name's Henry Arnold," the bigger man replied. "Care to tell me yours?"

Now it was Clint's turn to be surprised. Despite the reversal of fortune, the bigger man spoke without the slightest waver in his voice. Even more surprising was the fact that he looked as if he truly expected an answer.

"You want to lower that gun?" Clint asked.

After a moment's consideration, the man replied, "Depends on how you answer my question."

Since the horses he'd spotted before were still drawing closer, they took precedence in Clint's mind. "What about them?" he asked while hooking a thumb over his shoulder, toward the horses. "I don't suppose you know who they are?"

"Sure I do," Henry replied. "They're my reinforcements."

THREE

Clint stood his ground without moving a muscle. By the time the horses arrived, his gun arm was starting to ache and his knees were feeling the strain of keeping his stance beneath Henry's aim. Clint's only real comfort was that Henry seemed to be feeling more than a little strain of his own.

Well, it was also no small relief that Clint was fairly certain the bigger man wasn't going to pull his trigger. At least . . . not right away.

If Henry had meant to fire, he would have done so already. Even if he had intended on putting Clint to a test of speed and accuracy, Henry would have at least made a move to try to take a shot at Clint. All he would have needed to do was bend his elbow a little bit downward. Of course, if he did that, Clint would have just needed to tense his finger to burn a hole through Henry's midsection.

"Seems like we've got a situation here, Henry," Clint pointed out. "You think we can resolve it on our own, or do you need to wait for your cavalry to arrive?"

Henry smirked a bit and replied, "If you truly are the Gunsmith himself, I might need a cavalry."

"Not if we don't have any quarrel."

"We're both looking at each other over the barrel of a skinned gun. You don't count that as a quarrel?"

"Not yet."

Slowly, Henry nodded. He chewed on what he'd heard for a few more seconds, which was just enough time for the other horses to arrive. They thundered up to Clint's campsite as if they intended on trampling it into the ground. Amid a flurry of stomping hooves and loud whinnies, the horses were reined in and brought to a stop. By the time the whole group had gathered around the sputtering campfire, even Eclipse was getting nervous.

"You got him," declared a rider with wild eyes and close-cropped, dark blond hair. "Nice work, Henry."

"Hold on for a moment, Talman," Henry said. "This may not be the fella we're after."

Talman looked at Henry as if he'd just been told the sky was filled with polka dots. The grimace on his face twisted his patchy beard and revealed a gap where one of his front teeth should have been. Finally, he swung down from his saddle and spat a juicy wad of chewing tobacco onto the ground. "You found him right here, didn't you?"

"Yeah."

"And this ain't but a mile or so from the spot we found that shed."

"That don't mean this is the fella we're after," Henry said as he shook his head. So far, he had yet to take his eyes off Clint.

"Then why is your gun skinned?" Talman asked, looking around to the four horses and riders that had arrived alongside him. "Last time I checked, an innocent man ain't gonna pull his gun on a lawman."

"Lawman?" Clint asked.

Letting out a grunting laugh and then spitting another brown wad onto the ground, Talman said, "Too late to play dumb now, asshole." With that, he reached for the gun holstered at his side. Before he could clear leather, Talman was stopped by a sharp, barking voice.

"No!" Henry snapped. "Any of you men that draws your guns will answer to me, you hear? Any of you!"

There was plenty that Clint wanted to say. He had questions that needed answers and a few names to drop that might just carry some weight with lawmen. But Clint didn't say any of those things. Henry Arnold seemed to be doing a hell of a job on his own.

The four riders were a mix of young men and a few who'd seen more than their share of winters. All of them had their hackles up, but they weren't half as riled as Talman.

"What the hell's wrong with you, Henry?" Talman asked. "We've been looking for this murderous bastard and now we found him."

"How do you know it's him?" Henry asked.

"There ain't another soul for miles around that shed, and we find this one sitting here pretty as you please, downwind from those folks he cooked! Just look at him, for Christ's sake! He pulled a gun on you!"

Henry fixed his eyes on Clint and gave him an intent stare that was full of unspoken words. Even though Clint was fairly good at reading other people's faces, he didn't need years of experience at the poker table to know what Henry was after.

"I'm putting my gun down," Clint said. "See?"

Despite announcing his intentions, Clint still saw the other men flinch when he moved his gun arm. Talman snapped his gun toward Clint, while the four riders drew their weapons and took aim. Henry flinched as well, but he was mostly reacting to the other five.

Gritting his teeth and hoping for the best, Clint continued lowering his gun until the modified Colt touched against the ground. "There," he said after releasing the pistol from his grasp. "You see? We've got an honest mistake here, gentlemen. That's all."

Henry kept his stony expression more or less intact, but seemed plenty relieved as Clint lifted his arms into the air over his head.

Talman scoffed. "So he knows how to show us what we want to see. That don't prove a damned thing."

"Check his hands," Henry said. At the first sign of Talman moving toward Clint, Henry added, "Not you. Barkley. You check him."

Talman apparently knew better than to say anything, so he shook his head and muttered his comments to himself.

Barkley wasn't one of the younger riders, but he wasn't an

old man. Looking to be in his late forties, he had dark hair that was graying along the temple and sides of his head. He showed some experience with his job when he climbed from the saddle, walked over to Clint and began searching him without taking his eyes or his aim away from Clint for one second.

"He doesn't have any more weapons on him," Barkley said.

"The man we're after is a killer and he started a fire recently," Henry announced. "We know he stood by to watch it, so he'd have some trace of smoke on him or at least the smell of it sticking to him like glue."

"Could've changed his clothes," Talman added.

"Sure," Henry said with a nod. "Bower will check for that."

One of the younger riders responded to that name. A kid who couldn't have been more than a stone's throw from his twentieth birthday one way or another climbed down from his horse and rushed over to Clint's saddlebags. Once there, he rummaged through Clint's belongings.

Barkley took a closer look at Clint's face and hands. He even went so far as to look him straight in the eyes while pulling in a long breath. Finally, he shook his head. "I don't think this one's been around a fire as big as the one we're asking about."

"What about you, Bower?" Henry asked. "Find anything?"

Since Clint wasn't traveling with much, it hadn't taken the kid very long to sort through his things.

"There's some clothes and such, but they don't look like they been around no fire," Bower said.

The remaining two riders eased back into their saddles, but kept their guns aimed at Clint. Talman, on the other hand, wasn't so quick to lower his defenses.

"Could a buried his clothes," Talman said. "Could a washed up. Could a—"

"Could be he'll have more to say when we take him along with us," Henry interrupted. "Collect that gun of his and tie his hands, Barkley. Let's get moving. Don't forget we may still be looking for another killer."

Letting out a breath, Clint allowed his wrists to be tied together and his belongings to be taken. For the moment, he really didn't have another choice.

FOUR

Clint had been riding south through New Mexico for the last several days. Part of him had been enjoying the cool nights and the warmth of the sun on his face during the days. Another part of him had been relishing the fact that he'd escaped a nasty bout of snowstorms farther north. The last thing he'd expected was to find himself with his hands tied behind his back and surrounded by a bunch of supposed lawmen with twitchy trigger fingers.

At the moment, Clint rode on the back of one of the younger men's horses. The reins were being held by the horse's owner, who rode Eclipse directly in front of Clint. Actually, the younger man wasn't so much riding Eclipse as he was simply trying to keep moving while avoiding getting thrown by the Darley Arabian. Despite Clint's occasional words of comfort, the stallion wasn't any more happy with the situation than Clint was.

Although he was normally happy to oblige where the law was concerned, his patience was wearing thin. Having Talman eye him like he was a mangy dog didn't make Clint feel any more hospitable.

"Is anyone going to tell me what I'm supposed to be guilty of?" Clint asked. "Or should I guess?"

When no answer seemed to be forthcoming, Clint muttered, "Or perhaps I should just wait to be hanged?"

"There's the best notion I've heard all day," Talman grunted.

"Shut it," Henry warned.

Talman spat to one side and fixed his eyes on Clint. His hand rested on the grip of his pistol, and he made no attempt to hide the fact that he was aching to draw the pistol and put it to work.

With everyone trying to watch Clint while also trying to keep their eyes on their surroundings, it wasn't an easy ride. Fortunately, they weren't riding for long before Clint got an idea of what had brought them all to this spot in the first place.

His first hint was the scent of pungent smoke drifting through the air. Clint had smelled plenty of different kinds of fires, and most of them led to good things. Mostly, smoke told a man he was getting close to hot food, a warm room or at least a cup of hot coffee.

If the scent of smoke was too thick, it could mark a bad turn of events for a house or a section of town.

And then, every so often, the smell of smoke was mixed in with something that put a knot in a man's stomach.

When he'd sniffed that first trace of smoke, Clint had reflexively pulled some more of it into his lungs. Halfway through the second, deeper breath, Clint caught the distinctive odor of burning hair. It wasn't as powerful as the scents of charred wood, but the unmistakable odor stuck to the back of Clint's throat.

The scent of burned meat soon followed, and it was enough to make Clint happy he'd been captured before he'd eaten any breakfast.

"Jesus," Clint said. "Where the hell are you taking me?"

Talman turned around in his saddle to look at Clint. It was the first time he'd smiled. "We're downwind from your handiwork. Ain't so good from here, is it?"

"Shut up," Henry said. "Circle around before we trample any of those tracks we found."

The men obeyed without question. Even Talman took Henry's lead and came to a stop as soon as Henry gave the signal. Henry was the first to dismount, and the other men followed suit. Only Talman stayed in his saddle, so he could watch Clint over the barrel of his drawn pistol.

Walking directly over to Clint, Henry placed one hand on his holstered gun and his other on his hip. "What've you got to say for yourself?" he asked.

Clint couldn't take his eyes off the smoldering remains of the shed no more than twenty yards in front of him. The stench in the air seemed to grow thicker by the second, and the only thing that made him feel sicker was the thought of what could be causing it.

Shaking his head, Clint replied, "I don't know what to say."

After a few quiet seconds, Henry nodded. "Good enough for me." With that, he drew a knife from a scabbard at his belt and made a quick swipe at Clint.

Although Clint saw the blade flicker through the air, he barely even felt it touch his wrist. The only way he knew for certain the blade had made contact was the fact that the ropes binding his arms together were now severed.

"What in the hell?" Talman groused.

Placing the knife back into its sheath, Henry stepped back from Clint and said, "I told you once to shut up, Talman. I ain't about to tell you again."

"But for all we know he could be—"

"If he was the man we were after, he would've tried to make a move by now. He would've said something to tip his hand. Hell, he could have pulled his trigger on me before the rest of you got here and he would've been in the wind by now."

Shifting his gaze to the riders other than Talman, Henry said, "You men are all a part of this. Which of you still think this is the man who did this?"

The men glanced back at the smoking remains of the little building and then looked at Clint. Not one of them raised a hand or even gave half a nod.

Although Talman wasn't speaking up to defend himself, he still didn't look happy. "If he ain't the one, then that means we wasted all this time and let the other man get away."

Henry let out a slow, controlled sigh. His eyes were locked upon the charred shed. "Whoever did this was already long gone before we got here."

FIVE

Clint was on his feet, out of the ropes and not at the wrong end of anyone's gun. It felt good, but not half as good as when Henry stepped up to him and handed over Clint's modified Colt.

"Here you go," Henry said.

As Clint took the pistol, he could feel the eyes of all those other men upon him. Even though he was smiling and seemed genuine enough, Henry was showing some caution as well by keeping his other hand on the grip of his pistol.

Making sure to keep his movements slow, Clint took his gun and holstered it. Only after he'd moved his hand away from the Colt did he see some of the others relax a bit. Not only was Henry one of the ones to relax, but he was smirking and offering his open hand.

"Sorry about the trouble we caused you," Henry said. "It was an honest mistake."

When Clint started laughing at that, it was almost as much of a surprise to himself as it was to the rest of the men watching him. He shook Henry's hand and asked, "So is anyone going to tell me what this is all about?"

"Guess you've got a right to that. See that house there?"

"Doesn't look like it was big enough to be a house," Clint replied, "but yeah. I see it."

"That's the work of a man we've been after for a while."

"Not just one man," Talman added.

Henry nodded and said, "He's the one who figured that out, so he's also gotta remind everyone about it any chance he gets."

"And who are you men?" Clint asked. "Some sort of posse?"

"Not hardly," Henry replied. "We're Texas Rangers."

"Then I either got really lost or we were riding for a lot longer than I thought, because I thought this was New Mexico."

"It was. Still is, as a matter of fact. But the animal who set this fire started off in Texas. He's burned down plenty more homes in Texas. He's killed plenty of Texans. That means his hide belongs to us."

Clint wasn't exactly certain on the loopholes in the rules governing jurisdictional matters, but he wasn't about to second-guess Henry. The stern glare in Henry's eyes was mirrored in the eyes of all the other men, so Clint decided to let the matter be.

"Clint Adams," Henry said. "I've heard that name before."

"Hopefully what you heard was favorable," Clint said with a friendly grin.

"Mostly."

After spitting out a messy clump of tobacco, Talman said, "I heard of him, too. Heard he was a gunman and a killer."

Clint shifted his gaze to Talman. Although the Texas Ranger managed to lock eyes with Clint, he wasn't able to bear the full brunt of his stare for very long. When he looked away, Talman did so under the guise of spitting.

"I've gotten into more than my share of scrapes," Clint said evenly. "But I'll have words with any man who says I'm not allowed to defend myself if the situation arises."

Talman shifted on his feet and then looked at Barkley. "Plenty of men claim to be someone like the Gunsmith. That don't make it so."

"I don't know," Henry mused. "I've heard some good things. Namely from a saloon owner named Nick Hartford."

Clint smirked. "You're probably thinking about Rick

Hartman. He owns a place in Labyrinth. He may not be the only one in Texas to vouch for me, but he'd do it the loudest."

"That he would, Mr. Adams," Henry said.

"Now, if we're through with this song and dance," Clint grumbled, "I'd like to hear some more about the man you say set this fire. It smells like death around here. That means this place wasn't empty when it went up."

"That's right."

"I take it you or your men have already been inside?" Clint asked.

Henry found himself staring at the burned heap and then nodded. "Yeah. I been in there. Believe me when I tell you you don't want to see it for yourself."

Clint closed his eyes and bowed his head. "How many were inside?"

"Near as we could figure, there were three. We think they were women. Well, at least two of them were women. The other . . . well . . . there wasn't enough left to be certain."

Walking slowly toward the smoldering shed, Henry stared at the rubble as if he wasn't truly taking it in. Clint walked beside him, doing his best not to choke on the combined scents of smoke and the things that had been consumed by the flame. There was another scent in the air, which became more obvious the closer they got.

"Smells like kerosene was used," Clint said. "Lots of it."

"It was used here just like all the others."

"Jesus. And you say this has happened before?"

Henry nodded. "First one was outside of San Antonio. There was another a few miles east of Dallas. A few more a little closer to your neck of the woods in West Texas."

It took a moment for Clint to remember that they'd been talking about Rick Hartman's place in Labyrinth a few minutes ago. Rick's Place was in West Texas, but that seemed like a whole other world right about now.

"I've heard more than a few good things about you, Adams," Henry said. "And it came from more than just Rick Hartman. I know it's not my place to ask, but I'd be obliged if—"

"If you're asking if I could lend you a hand in tracking

down whoever set these fires," Clint interrupted, "you don't need to ask. The animal who did this needs to be found, and I want to take part in it."

"And what if we don't need your help?" Talman asked.

Clint turned to once again stare down the man with the tobacco-stained smirk. "Then you're going to have to get me to leave. I promise it won't be as easy as when I let you handle me before."

Talman steeled himself, but he still wasn't able to keep his chin up for long.

Rather than push his advantage too far, Clint looked away first. "So who do you think did this?" he asked after glancing toward Henry.

The leader of the Rangers slowly shook his head and muttered, "Whoever it was, he's a goddamn monster."

SIX

A woman lay upon a bed with her blouse pulled open and her legs spread wide. Her hair was splayed out behind her and her eyes were glimmering like two jewels embedded in her head. She kept her arms out to her sides and her wrists pressed against the mattress well before they were pushed down by a pair of thick, scarred hands.

The man who climbed on top of her already had his shirt off and his belt unbuckled. After straddling her waist, he rubbed his groin between her legs and showed her a wide, glistening smile.

"That's right, baby," the woman said. "Just like that."

His name was Voorhees. Although he'd come from a family using that same name, he didn't need to use his first name. There wasn't much confusion since he'd killed off the rest of his family several years ago. But Voorhees wasn't thinking about his family. He was more preoccupied with the soft breasts he was fondling and the warmth pressed up against his growing erection.

Voorhees fumbled with her body as if it was the first time he'd ever touched her. All the while, he grinned and struggled to say what he was thinking. Instead, the only sounds he could make were grunts and groans. His head was swimming amid a flurry of sights and textures. His blood was pumping too fast for him to focus.

Seeing the frustration on his face, the woman reached up to place her hands upon his chest. "Shhh," she whispered as she eased him back and off of her. "Let me do it."

The moment Voorhees felt his back touch the mattress, he was able to let out the breath that had snagged in his throat.

"Is that better?" she asked.

"Yes, Elizabeth," Voorhees replied. "Much better."

Elizabeth smiled and straddled him. Her back straightened, and she peeled off her blouse as if she was simply brushing away a cobweb. Looking down upon his face, she licked her lips and then sifted her fingers through her hair.

For the first few seconds, Voorhees kept himself from touching her. He reached out for her hips and then for her breasts, but pulled away as if he was afraid of being scolded. Once his hand came to rest upon her leg, he clenched his jaw and grabbed onto her.

"That's the way," Elizabeth whispered. "Just like that."

At first, Voorhees rubbed her leg fervently. Then, his hand made its way under her bunched-up skirts and dug all the way up until he could feel the thatch of hair between her legs. He slipped the tips of two fingers into her, causing Elizabeth to arch her back and shudder on top of him.

"Did you do that for me?" she asked.

Voorhees didn't reply. He slid his fingers in and out of her, savoring the way she shook and trembled with an approaching orgasm.

"The fire," Elizabeth moaned through gritted teeth. "Did you set that fire for me?"

"Yes," Voorhees whispered. "Just for you."

Elizabeth's eyes snapped open, and she reached for the front of his jeans so she could pull them down viciously. She couldn't free his erection fast enough, and she wrapped her fingers around it. Stroking him up and down, she got him even harder before finally lifting herself up and taking him inside of her.

"Yes," she moaned as she rode back and forth along the length of his penis. "You set all of them for me, didn't you?"

Grabbing onto her hips, Voorhees moved her even faster while pumping up into her. "Every one of them, Elizabeth. Every goddamn one."

As she listened to him, Elizabeth dug her fingernails into Voorhees's chest. As her orgasm swiftly approached, she dug her nails in even harder, until she finally drew blood. Before tearing into him any more, Elizabeth leaned back and braced herself with her arms against his legs. From there, she writhed on top of him until every inch of her body was gripped in a powerful climax.

When Voorhees reached out for her, his fingers were curled into the shape of meaty claws. Although he scraped his nails against her skin for an inch or so, he eased up once he was touching the sensitive skin of her clitoris. Then, he rubbed her sweet spot with his thumb and watched as she squirmed and tried desperately to catch her breath.

It took a while for her to regain her strength, but she was eventually able to straighten up and ride him properly. Her head drooped forward, and she needed to place her hands upon his chest to keep herself upright. Elizabeth closed her eyes and rocked on top of him, riding his cock slowly and insistently.

Voorhees kept rubbing her. He could feel her getting wetter and wetter the more he rubbed, which allowed him to glide in and out of her even easier. Soon, she merely had to pump her hips to put a wide smile on his face.

The haze in Voorhees's eyes had cleared. He was breathing easier, and the muscles were no longer jumping beneath his skin. Before too much longer, he was able to sit up and roll Elizabeth onto her back. He then pushed her legs apart and settled in between them. His rigid cock fit perfectly into her, and she accepted every inch of it with a grateful sigh.

"Oh yes," she moaned. "Do it for me."

Voorhees placed both hands upon her breasts and thrust between her thighs. He thrust into her until Elizabeth was panting with exhaustion. He kept on pumping until he exploded inside of her. The pleasure he felt was enough to make him ball up his fist and pull it back almost as far as his ear.

Recognizing the way his muscles tensed, Elizabeth turned her head before his fist came down. Voorhees punched the mattress hard enough to jostle her whole body on impact. Still, it was better than the alternative.

Elizabeth looked at the fist that was still pressing down into the mattress beside her and smiled warmly. "Are you gonna do it again for me, baby?" she asked.

Slowly shifting his eyes away from her, Voorhees got the same faraway look in his eyes that showed up when he was looking at a raging fire. "Soon," he growled. "I'll do it again real soon."

SEVEN

"Looks like these tracks headed in from the south," Clint said as he hunkered down for a closer look at the ground near the burned shed. "And then they circle around to head back in the same direction."

"Coming or going, they only take us about a quarter of a mile in that direction before disappearing," Barkley said.

Standing a little ways back from the shed, Henry added, "And if you can believe anyone who tells you some tracks disappear, you can believe Barkley."

Clint looked over to the man who seemed to be one of the older members of the group of Texas Rangers. He had the keen eyes and grizzled appearance of an experienced trapper. Judging by the way he carried himself and the guns strapped to his waist, he may have even tangled with a bear or two in his day.

"How'd you find this place?" Clint asked.

"Little bit of know-how," Barkley replied. "Mixed in with a little bit of luck. Mostly, this killer sets his fires and then moves along. He seemed to be following a broken-down old trail that led out of Texas, so we followed that trail after we lost his tracks."

"Looks like two separate sets of tracks to me," Clint added.

Barkley nodded. "Yeah, but they pretty much act like one.

Whenever we've spotted tracks at a fire, there've been two sets of them. There were even two sets of tracks that we followed out of Texas."

"And you stumbled upon this?"

"Least we didn't sleep like a baby a stone's throw from where good folks were dying," Talman grunted.

There was no mistaking the barbed edge to Talman's voice, but Clint didn't get too rattled by it. Instead, he glanced toward Talman and stated, "True, but I didn't know this killer was about. What's your excuse for what happened here?"

Talman started to lunge forward, but was stopped by Henry's outstretched hand.

"Did you see what you needed to see here, Adams?" Henry asked. "Because we can't let any more time slip by."

"Agreed," Clint said as he dusted himself off and turned his back to the shed. "Whoever did this can't be too far away. My guess is they're holed up at the nearest town."

Henry squinted and asked, "You don't think they'd keep running?"

"How many fires have there been?" Clint asked.

After a slight pause, Henry replied, "Too many."

"Then . . . no offense . . . but I'd say these killers are pretty certain they've got you and your men figured out. They may have been running at first, but they might just be getting lazy right about now. Or, if not lazy, pretty confident in their chances of keeping ahead of you."

Talman started to grunt a string of obscenities directed at Clint, but was stopped once again by Henry. This time, the Rangers' leader used his outstretched arm to thump Talman in the chest.

"I don't wanna hear it, Talman," Henry snarled. "Clint's right. And this ain't a bad thing."

Clint nodded quickly. "That's for damn sure. The best fight you can get into is with someone who's too confident for their own good."

"Too bad they had to earn that confidence through so many folks getting killed," Bower said.

Turning toward the younger Ranger, Clint said, "I'd have

to agree. I passed through a town not too far west of here. Is that the closest one?"

"No," Barkley said. "There's another one due north. Actually, it may be about the same distance as the one you're thinking of."

"Then let's split up," Henry suggested. "Me, Clint, Bower and Dave will head west. The rest of you boys head north."

When Clint heard that other name mentioned, he glanced over at the other Texas Rangers who'd been content to hang back and stay quiet. Those two glared right back at him, making it obvious why they'd stayed quiet and out of Clint's sight. Apparently, Henry was a man who liked to cover himself when he took a gamble on a new addition to his group.

"Actually," Clint said, "maybe some of you should stay here."

Clint figured that suggestion wouldn't go over too well with all the Rangers, and he was right.

Talman looked as if he was about to bust out of his skin. "Oh, that sounds like a fine idea. You sure you want to let this one tag along, Henry?"

Although Henry didn't join in with Talman right away, he did look at Clint with more than a little expectation in his eyes. "Go on, Clint," Henry said. "I'm listening."

"I've tracked down a lot of killers over the years," Clint explained. "I've even gotten to know a few of them."

"Jesus Christ," Talman muttered. "Here we go."

"If the killers who started these fires are doing the same thing everywhere they go, they've got to be doing it on purpose. Even animals don't just attack whatever crosses their path. There's rhyme and reason."

Talman shook his head and spat on the ground. "This sounds like the biggest pile of horse shit I've ever heard."

"No, it doesn't," Barkley said.

It seemed the tracker's stern tone carried plenty of weight among the Rangers, because not even Talman was anxious to go against him.

Taking advantage of the opening he'd been given, Clint continued. "A killer may not be right in the head, and I'd say that's got to be the case here, but they've still got their reasons."

"So why stay here?" Barkley asked.

"Because these killers obviously like what they do," Clint replied. "They take some pleasure in it, otherwise they wouldn't keep killing this way. If they like setting these fires and are getting overly confident, they may just want to come back and soak this place in some more."

"Fruits of their labors, huh?" Henry asked.

Clint pointed at the leader of the Rangers. "Exactly. You've got all these men with you, so you might as well put them all to work. That is, unless you think it'll take all of us to get a look at those two towns."

"It could be useful to have us all sifting through those towns . . ."

"Thank you," Talman said victoriously.

Staring daggers at Talman, Henry went on to say, ". . . but I also think Clint's right. It couldn't hurt to leave a few of you here while we're away. We've come this far, so it doesn't make sense to pass up any opportunity we may get to catch these sons of bitches."

"If you want me to stay so your men can head to town, I'd be more than happy to oblige," Clint offered.

Henry didn't need to ponder that for too long before shaking his head. "I think you may be more useful coming along with us. There's more of a chance we'll be seen in town, and I've gotten the feeling those killers have seen the faces of me and my men."

"I'd bet on it," Barkley said.

"You're not one of my men, so the sight of you might not put the killers on their guard. Hopefully, they won't find out you're working with me."

"So he's working with us now?" Talman asked. "He gave us an opinion here and all, but he's coming along for more?"

"Sure," Henry replied. "If he doesn't mind lending a hand."

"I'll see what I can do while I'm here," Clint said.

Talman rolled his eyes and turned away from the others. "Great," he mumbled. "Just great."

EIGHT

Clint didn't know exactly why Henry decided on taking him and Talman both into the northern town, but he could only assume it was to keep him where both he and Talman could see him. Either that, or Henry enjoyed listening to Talman spit insults at Clint whenever he wasn't spitting brown juice onto the ground.

Bower went to the second town with one of the other Rangers who Clint didn't recall saying much of anything. That left Barkley and Dave to find a spot near the burned shed where they could watch the charred remains without being seen.

While Clint might have preferred to be in one of the other groups, he supposed he could understand Henry's reasoning. Since he was the unknown factor Henry was dealing with, it only made sense that he'd be under close supervision until he proved himself. Still, that didn't mean Clint had to enjoy Talman's company.

Clint had ridden through these parts enough times to know where the larger towns were and to have a good idea where some of the smaller ones could be found. He'd picked out a few little places as his personal favorites throughout the years, but the town he, Henry and Talman rode into this time didn't fall into any of those categories.

The place wasn't a large town. It wasn't anywhere Clint had been to before, and it sure didn't seem like it would be on his list for a return visit. As it was, he felt like doing what needed to be done and then putting it behind him.

"Well," Talman grunted as he glanced in either direction upon entering the town. "This place looks like a hole in the ground."

Clint chuckled. "Finally, there's something we can agree on."

"Yeah, well before you two get too cozy, I want us to split up," Henry said. "I'd rather not be spotted by those killers if they're here, and I surely don't want them to see us and Clint riding together. That'd ruin what little bit of surprise we got working for us."

"Agreed," Clint said. "I see a hotel and a saloon up ahead. I'll meet up with you at the saloon tonight after ten or so. That should give us some time to have a look around."

Talman snapped his reins and tossed a quick wave over his shoulder. "Fine. Try not to get yourself burned up, Adams."

With that, Talman and Henry moved on to leave Clint behind. The two Rangers tossed a few words back and forth, but their voices were too low for Clint to make out what was said. That suited him just fine, since he was glad to have some peace and quiet for a stretch.

With a subtle pull of the reins, Clint slowed Eclipse down to a leisurely stroll. He let the Darley Arabian mosey into town so the other two men could get well ahead of him. That way, Clint could get a better look at the town from his perspective. Hopefully, he could look at the place from someone else's perspective as well.

The place was small, which meant no stranger would go unnoticed for very long. Of course, if someone was to get on a local's good side quickly enough, he might be able to get some measure of protection that would make escaping much easier.

The town also seemed fairly easy to ditch if push came to shove. Along those same lines, a town that size probably didn't have much by way of law. Most likely, there was some lawman who'd sat behind his desk for so many years that he didn't even bother making his rounds every night. On the other hand, the law could be enforced by some young man who didn't have much experience elsewhere. Either way, it was a good place for a killer to hide.

After seeing the remains of that shed and the bodies inside, Clint didn't intend on letting that killer get too far.

"All right," Clint said to himself as he gave Eclipse's reins a snap. "Let's see what we can see."

He rode down what must have been the town's main street. Henry and Talman must have taken full advantage of their head start, because they were nowhere to be seen. Even though it had been less than a minute or so since he and Talman had parted ways, Clint was already feeling better.

Now the best he could hope for was to keep his ride with the rogue Texas Rangers as short as possible. That would mean putting these killers out of business as quickly as possible. After what he'd seen of the killers' handiwork, Clint couldn't get to work fast enough.

NINE

Sometimes, a town's saloon was better than its newspaper. There were plenty of times when a town built several saloons before even considering starting up a printing press. This time, looking at the saloon's front window was all Clint needed to do in order to find out where he was. The town's name was Kipperway, and apparently it had been founded less than three years ago.

Stepping through the front door of the Kipperway Tavern, Clint felt like he'd stumbled into a whole other place entirely. Compared to the dead quiet of the street, the inside of the saloon was busting with life. The bar may have been crooked, but that was mostly because there were over a dozen men leaning against it. A piano player sent a wobbly tune through the air, and there was even a stage close to the front door. All in all, Clint had to admit he was impressed.

"Good day to you, sir," the lanky fellow behind the bar shouted. His voice cut through the noise like a knife and was colored by a thick Irish accent. "What brings you to my little tavern?"

"Nothing in particular," Clint said. "But I'm glad I found this place."

"And I'm glad to have ya. You care for a beer? I brewed it myself."

"Sure."

Clint didn't have to wait long for a mug to be brought to him. Once it was set down in front of him, he took a sip and was surprised for the second time in as many minutes.

"Damn," Clint said. "That's really good. You brewed this?"

"Sure did. An old family recipe." Leaning forward, the bartender gave Clint a nudge and a wink as he whispered, "Actually, I worked it out myself a week ago, but don't tell anyone else that."

"I don't care if you found the recipe under a rock. This is some damn fine beer."

Beaming proudly, the bartender straightened up and wiped off the bar. "Anything else I can get you?"

"Actually, I'd like to know if you've seen any other strangers come through here recently."

"Strangers?"

"Yeah. I lost track of some friends of mine and I think they may have come through here."

The bartender's face darkened and he let out a worried breath. "Your friends didn't go to the Wilkins place by any chance, did they?"

"I don't think so. Why?"

"Because there was some bad things happening out there," the bartender said with a wince. "Place burned right down to the ground, and we think it took the Wilkins folks with it."

"You think?"

"They kept mostly to themselves. Just stayed out there on their own and only came to town when they needed supplies and such. Since they been to town less than a week ago, nobody was expectin' them back soon. For all we know, they could have just packed up and left for somewhere."

Clint took another sip of his beer and shrugged. "Didn't anyone go out to check?"

The barkeep thought about that for a few seconds before saying, "Not as such."

"Then how do you know there was a fire?"

"Someone mentioned it."

"Who?" The moment he asked that question, Clint could feel the suspicions arising within the barkeep's head. He adjusted to it reflexively, as if he was trying to cover up a slip of the tongue at a card table. "If my friends did head out that way, I'd sure like to know."

That seemed to be enough to staunch the barkeep's reservations. "Why don't you ask Belle over there?" he said. "She's the one who told me about it."

Clint looked in the direction the barkeep was pointing and spotted more than a few women in the vicinity.

As if sensing the next question on Clint's mind, the barkeep added, "She's the one with her hair tied up in the ribbons."

"Good," Clint said with a grin. "I was hoping she was the one you meant. I appreciate the help."

"Not a problem, mister. Hope to see more of you around here."

"I'm sure you will."

"And I hope you find your friends."

Clint only partially heard that last bit since he was focused completely on the woman that had been singled out.

She seemed slightly taller than average, but it was hard to tell since she was leaning against the back wall. Although her dark hair was most definitely tied up in ribbons as the bartender had mentioned, it wasn't the first thing that caught Clint's attention. Considering that she wore a dress with a neckline low enough to display a beautiful pair of firm breasts, it was a wonder any man could notice those ribbons.

Her lips were full and had a natural redness to them that made a man instantly wonder what they tasted like. The way she talked and smiled, it seemed pretty safe to say that she knew exactly how sweet her lips were. Holding a whiskey bottle in one hand, she set her eyes on Clint and ran the tip of her thumb along the neck of her bottle.

"Hello," Clint said as he approached her. "Are you Belle?"

She smiled and nodded. "That's me. Who might you be?"

Before Clint could respond, he saw the man next to Belle reach out and shove him with the flat of his hand. At least, he would have shoved him if Clint hadn't reflexively batted the man's hand away before it touched him.

"Find another place to stand, mister," the man said.

Clint sized up the other man in the space of a heartbeat. He was about Clint's height, with just enough meat on his bones to make him think others should step aside for him. Just to back up the ugly sneer on his face, the man wore two guns and a knife hanging from the belts wrapped around his waist.

"Don't be so cross, Red," Belle said before Clint could make a move. "Just give me a moment and I'll come right back to you."

Red's mouth hung open, and he hardly seemed to notice that Belle had spoken.

"I won't take long, Red," Clint said. "I promise."

"You'd better not," Red grunted. As he walked away, he made certain to knock Clint's shoulder with his own.

Once Red had stepped away, Clint looked to Belle and tipped his hat. "My name's Clint. I just wanted to ask you about what happened at the Wilkins place."

"Are you friends of theirs?" Belle asked.

"Yeah," Clint replied, figuring that going after someone's killers would qualify him as a friend. "It's been a long time since I've seen them, though."

"I'm so sorry," Belle said earnestly. "There was a fire. I saw it myself."

"You saw the fire?"

She nodded. "I live a ways away from them, but it happened in the middle of the night and I could see the flames. I don't know what happened to those folks, but I did see someone poking around that place a little while before the fire."

Trying not to look too interested, Clint asked, "You did? Was it one of the Wilkins?"

"I don't think so. They rode a horse, and the folks who lived there only traveled about in a wagon on account of their age."

"I see. Anything else you could tell me?"

After thinking it over for a few seconds, Belle shook her head. "No. I didn't see much else. Like I told you, it was dark."

"All right, then. I appreciate your time."

When Clint started to leave, he felt Belle's hand wrap

around his elbow. He allowed himself to be turned around so he could see her smiling face.

"Sorry about earlier with Red and all," she said. "He's not from around here."

"Neither am I," Clint said.

"Yeah, but I can tell you're more like the folks from these parts." Sliding her hand along Clint's chest and letting it linger near his belt buckle, she added, "We're real friendly."

"I can . . . uh . . . see that."

"I can show you some more if you like."

"Sounds tempting. Maybe I'll see you around here a little later."

"Oh, you sure will," Belle said with a warm, promising smile.

As Clint left the saloon, he was still thinking about Belle's full lips and the last smile she'd shown him. Perhaps that was why he didn't see Red taking a swing at him until it was too late to duck.

TEN

Red's knuckles cracked against Clint's jaw and sent him sidestepping away from the saloon's front door. As he stepped forward, Red shook out the pain in his hand while grinning like he'd just won a prize.

"Maybe you should go back to wherever you came from," Red grunted.

Playing on the confidence in Red's voice, Clint kept his head down and leaned against the saloon. Once Red had strutted close enough, Clint balled up his own fist and sent it Red's way. His punch didn't make as much noise as Red's, but it drove far enough into the man's gut that he doubled over.

"I'm sure Belle's real impressed," Clint said. "Now go back inside while you're still able."

Red coughed and gritted his teeth. "That's the last mistake you're gonna make," he said, and he rushed toward Clint with both arms held open.

Now that Clint was ready for it, he evaded Red's attack easily enough. All he needed to do was raise his arms and turn to one side to allow Red to stumble past him. For good measure, Clint dropped one of his elbows between Red's shoulder blades.

As he ran toward a nearby post, Red let out a frustrated

snarl and dug his heels in to stop himself. When he wheeled around, he found Clint standing in the spot where he'd left him, with his shoulders squared.

"What the hell did you want to know about that place that burnt down?" Red snapped.

Clint had been expecting plenty from Red, but that question wasn't one of them. "What did you say?" Clint asked.

Seeing the surprise on Clint's face, Red stopped just outside of Clint's reach and replied, "You heard me. Why the hell were you askin' about that place?"

"What business is it of yours?"

"Don't you worry about that, mister. Just steer clear of it." With that, Red drew his pistol. Before he could take aim, he saw Clint take a few steps forward.

"What do you know about that place?" Clint asked.

"It's mine, you hear? Mine!"

Clint kept his eyes locked on Red. He stared him down until he'd moved in just close enough to reach out and snatch the gun from Red's hand in a single blur of motion. If Clint's jaw hadn't still been aching from that first punch, he would have smiled at the look of shock on Red's face.

Holding Red's gun by the barrel, Clint locked eyes again with the man. Whether it was out of bravery, stupidity or just plain stubbornness, Red would not look away. Finally, Clint flipped the gun around so he could empty the cylinder with a few practiced movements of his fingers.

With every bullet that hit the ground, Red seemed to get madder. When Clint snapped the cylinder back into place and handed the gun to its owner, Red took it with a trembling hand.

"Sorry for your loss," Clint said.

It was a short walk back into the saloon. Every step of the way, Clint listened to Red's scrambling as the man scraped the bullets from the ground and fumbled to reload his pistol. Fortunately, Red was still angry and shaking enough to hamper his ability to fit the rounds properly into the chambers.

"Do yourself a favor," Clint said before walking into the saloon. "Don't let me see you skin that pistol again. I won't be feeling so generous the next time."

When Clint stepped back into the saloon, he found most of the people at or near the bar watching him. One of those people was Henry, and he didn't look too happy. Before Clint could make his way over to the Texas Ranger's table, he saw another familiar face. To say this one was more appealing than Henry's would have been an understatement.

"I want to thank you for getting him away from me," Belle said as she walked over to Clint. Before he could reply, she wrapped her arms around him and gave him a kiss.

Reluctantly, Clint eased away from her so he could get a look at Belle's face. "What was that for again?"

"For letting me get the hell away from Red. He was about to pull me out of here any moment."

"Really?"

"That's what it felt like. Anyway, you're much better company."

Clint took her hand and led her to one of the few vacant spots inside the saloon. All of the tables were more or less occupied, but there was a corner toward the back that suited his purpose. He didn't have to see Henry's face to know the Texas Ranger wasn't happy about that move.

"What did Red want from you?" Clint asked.

Belle shrugged. "What do most men want from me?"

"Not that. It had something to do with the Wilkins place."

She furrowed her brow a bit and told him, "He asked about it, but I didn't have much to say. I didn't even tell him as much as I told you."

"What did he ask?"

"Just what was left and if anyone else was looking around."

"And what did you tell him?"

"Now you're starting to scare me." Shaking her head, she began to turn away from him while muttering, "Maybe I should just leave this place before tangling with another man."

"Red pulled a gun on me outside," Clint said. "It seemed like it had something to do with what happened at the Wilkins place."

That caused Belle to stop and turn around to face him. "Well, you can take it up with him. He's staying at the hotel. I know because he invited me back there with him. By the sound of it, he was going to be there until dark and then he was heading out somewhere. Before you ask, I don't know where he was headed."

Clint nodded. "Thanks. I appreciate it."

Letting out a frustrated sigh, Belle spun around and left Clint in a huff.

ELEVEN

Clint arrived at Henry's table carrying two mugs. As he sat down, he placed the mugs on the table.

"What's this?" Henry asked.

"Beer," Clint replied simply. "It's really good."

Henry took the mug as if he thought it might nip at his hand. When it didn't, he lifted it to his mouth and took a sip. In a matter of seconds, he was grinning and nodding. "That is good. Sure is better than the piss water these places usually serve."

"Where's Talman?"

"Hopefully he's following that fella who tried to knock your head off not too long ago."

"You saw that, huh?" Clint asked.

"Oh yeah."

"Thanks for stepping in. I'll bet Talman really enjoyed the show."

Despite the fact that Henry obviously knew something on that matter, he didn't bother sharing it with Clint. Instead, he asked, "What was the cause of that scuffle?"

"The man out there with me is named Red. I thought he was just trying to catch a lady's eye, but it's more than that."

"You sure?" Henry asked as he watched Belle wind her way through the crowd. "That's quite a lady."

"Jesus, you were in here for the start of that fight, too?"

"No, but Talman was. He may be a pain in the ass, but he's good at his job."

"Anyway," Clint went on to say, "Red's got an interest in the place that was burnt down."

"You think he may be the fellow we're after?" Henry asked.

Reluctantly, Clint shrugged. "I don't know. He sure seems to take offense in me asking around about it. He's staying at the hotel."

Henry nodded. "I know. We saw him head that way after you taught him his lesson outside. Talman's trailing him right now."

Clint looked around at the crowd filling up the saloon. Although there were plenty of people nearby, none of them seemed too interested in what Clint and Henry were doing. Even if they were, it was loud enough in there to cover up the two men's voices.

"I think we should all keep an eye on him," Clint said. "It sounds like he may be riding somewhere tonight, and we don't want to lose sight of him."

"Where's he going?"

After taking a drink of his beer, Clint replied, "I don't know for certain, but Red might even be heading out sooner rather than later, after the conversation I had with him earlier."

Henry grumbled to himself as he looked into his mug and swirled the beer around. "I thought we were after more than one man."

"Red doesn't strike me as the sort who would work all by himself."

"Does he strike you as a killer?"

Without hesitation, Clint nodded. "He drew his gun, and he would have pulled the trigger if I hadn't stopped him. Even if he's not the man we're after, he's got some sort of interest in the place that was burned down. That's got to count for something."

"It counts for a hell of a lot," Henry said as he pushed

back from the table and stood up. "Let's see if Talman has anything to add to this situation."

Casting a few nervous glances around the room, Clint asked, "Do you care who sees me working with you?"

"Hell no, I don't care who sees!" Henry bellowed. "The next time you decide to stir up that kind of fight in the middle of the street, you'd better think twice!"

At first, Clint was surprised by Henry's outburst. Although it didn't take long for him to figure out what the Texas Ranger was doing, Clint kept the shocked expression on his face. Judging by the looks on the faces of the other people within earshot, Henry was doing a fine job of explaining their conversation to any interested parties.

Just to put some icing on the cake, Henry shot a murderous glare at Clint before stomping out of the saloon. By the time he'd left the place, most everyone else inside had already gotten back to their own affairs.

Clint was about to sit down when he noticed one man in the saloon who was staring at him for a bit longer than the rest. The man was a big fellow with coarse skin that resembled the floor of a desert. Rather than avert his eyes, he let them drift away to settle on one of the ladies moving through the crowd.

As he left the saloon, Clint watched the man with the rough face. The man didn't make any sudden moves or do anything too suspicious, but that didn't keep Clint's nerves from jangling inside of him.

Once he stepped outside, Clint couldn't help but feel like he'd made a mistake in turning his back on the man with the rough face. Knowing better than to second-guess his instincts, Clint turned right back around and pulled open the saloon's door.

Belle rushed toward him, so Clint took a step inside so his view wouldn't be blocked by the woman.

"I was hoping you hadn't left," she said breathlessly. "I wanted to tell you something."

Clint put his hands on her shoulders and moved her aside so he could get a look at the table where the rough-faced man had been. He picked it out before too long, but it was too late. The table was empty.

The moment he saw that empty chair, Clint swore under his breath. He then turned around and left the saloon for good. He swore at himself again for wasting as much time as he already had.

TWELVE

Clint rushed to the hotel and went straight to the front desk.

The man behind the desk looked to be somewhere in his fifties and dressed in his Sunday best. Straightening a string tie, the man asked, "What can I do for y—"

"Two men checked into this hotel recently," Clint interrupted without caring who else might be listening. "Where are they?"

"Are you a friend or family?"

Not wanting to get into an entire conversation, Clint grabbed the register from the desk and took a look at the most recent entry. While Henry or Talman's names weren't on there, he did see two signatures. The only ones other than those had been written several days before.

The two newest arrivals were marked down for room numbers one and two. Sure enough, when Clint looked up to the hooks on the wall behind the clerk's head, the keys to those two rooms were the only ones missing.

The clerk was still trying to get Clint's attention even after Clint had headed for the stairs leading to the second floor. Clint didn't care what the clerk was trying to say. All he could think about was catching up with one or both of the Texas Rangers as soon as possible.

Unfortunately, Clint caught up to the one he'd been hoping to avoid.

"What the hell are you doin' here?" Talman asked as he pulled open the door to room number one and stuck his head outside. "You're supposed to keep your distance."

"Where's Henry?" Clint asked.

"Supposed to be with you. What's the problem?"

"We need to get back to the spot where that fire was."

"Huh?" Talman asked. "Why?"

"I'll explain along the way. Right now, we just need to get moving."

Although he didn't seem any more pleased to work with Clint, Talman stepped outside and shut the door behind him. "Let's get the horses," he said. "We should cross paths with Henry somewhere along the way."

Clint turned on the balls of his feet and headed for the stairs again. He nearly walked straight over the hotel's clerk, who was on his way up. As before, Clint handily ignored the flustered man.

"What's the meaning of this?" the clerk sputtered to the back of Clint's head. Turning toward Talman, he snapped, "I didn't have any part in this intrusion. In fact I—"

But Talman had already stomped down the stairs past the clerk, leaving the older man scratching his chin and looking around as if he'd been narrowly missed by a speeding train. Shrugging his shoulders, the clerk headed downstairs again and stepped behind his desk.

Outside, Talman and Clint only had to take two steps onto the boardwalk before catching sight of Henry.

"What the hell are you two doing here?" Henry growled. "I thought you'd know I was trying to make it look like—"

"I know what you were doing in the saloon," Clint interrupted. "But we need to get to that shed."

"Why? I thought you said we had some time before that Red fellow headed out that way."

"I think he may be moving sooner than that," Clint replied. "And I saw someone in the saloon that didn't look right. Every bone in my body is just telling me to get back out there right now."

After thinking it over for a second or two, Henry nodded. "Fine. You and I will go. Talman, you'll stay here."

"Why should I stay?" Talman protested.

"Because you're the one that's been seen the least. That is, unless you count right now. So get away from us and search this town top to bottom until you find that fellow that called Clint out of that saloon earlier."

Despite the fact that he obviously had plenty more on his mind, Talman knew better than to try to say his piece right then and there. Instead, he turned his back to the other two and waved them off as he stepped back into the hotel.

"Go on and get your horse," Henry said. "I'll catch up to you."

Clint ran back to the post where he'd tied Eclipse and then jumped into the saddle. The Darley Arabian was only too eager to bolt from Kipperway like an arrow that had been shot from a bow. As promised, Henry thundered up alongside Clint, and the two of them raced to the spot where they'd left two of Henry's men.

THIRTEEN

After staring at the charred remains of the shed for so many hours, Barkley hardly even thought about the fact that good folks had been burned alive in there. The blackened pile of lumber was just another part of the landscape now.

The world kept turning.

There was still work to be done.

When he heard the rumble of horses approaching at full gallop, Barkley lifted his head just enough to get a look at the northern horizon.

"You hear that?" Barkley's partner asked.

Dave was a good man, but the main thing that had gotten him into the Texas Rangers was his father's connections. While he didn't do much to distinguish himself as a Ranger, Dave never appreciated his father steering his life. Perhaps that was why he'd volunteered to join up with Henry on this ride out of the Rangers' jurisdiction.

Barkley looked over at the other Ranger while also thinking about these couple of things. Even with those points considered, he couldn't hide the contempt on his face that someone like Dave was riding alongside a good bunch of trackers, lawmen and manhunters.

"Yeah," Barkley said. "I heard it."

"You think it's Henry or Bower coming back?"

"Bower would be coming from the west. Remember?"

Dave nodded quickly. "I remember. I just . . . Who are those men? There's more than there should be."

Having been walking over to his saddlebags to retrieve his telescope, Barkley raised the instrument to his eye and peered through the lenses. Strangely enough, Dave had a point. It surprised Barkley so much that he had to check what he saw a second time.

"You're right," Barkley admitted. "There should only be three of them at the most. I count five."

"You think Henry caught that killer and is bringing him back?"

Barkley kept staring through the telescope before shaking his head. "I don't think so."

"Then maybe someone else is coming to have a look at this place."

"Yeah. Could be. Best get your rifle in case they're not in a sociable sort of mood."

Dave wore a look of concern on his face, but didn't hesitate before doing what he was told. He got his rifle and walked back to where Barkley was standing. The tracker already had taken his own rifle from where it hung from his saddle and propped it against his hip.

"What if those folks are just . . . family?" Dave asked. "You know. Family of who was in that shed and they're just coming to check on them."

"Then we won't shoot."

Dave held his rifle in both hands and faced the same direction as Barkley. As the horses drew closer, Dave shifted uncomfortably from one foot to another. Squinting at the approaching riders, he focused on one of them moving in a peculiar way. When he turned to say as much to Barkley, Dave was just in time to see Barkley get knocked to one side as if he was swatted by an unseen fist.

A second or so later, the report of a rifle echoed in the distance.

"Jesus Christ!" Dave shouted as he dropped to one knee next to his fallen partner.

Barkley let out a pained snarl through gritted teeth as he

pulled himself back up. As soon as he was upright again, he brought his rifle to his shoulder and fired off a round.

Dave turned to see if he could pick out a target and found that the other riders had covered even more distance than he'd guessed. The shock on his face remained as he lent his own fire to the shots Barkley was putting into the air.

Levering in a fresh round, Barkley grunted, "Shit. They're splitting up."

Sure enough, Dave watched as the riders fanned out and broke into two groups. One of the groups headed to the left of the shed and the other steered toward the right. No more shots had come from the riders, but that didn't seem to make either of the Rangers feel too good.

"They're flanking us!" Barkley shouted over the ringing in his ears that had been put there by all the rifle fire.

"What do we do?" Dave asked.

"We sure as hell don't stand here and wait for them to close in." Taking a quick look behind him, Barkley was glad to see neither of their horses had been spooked by the noise. "Mount up and get moving. The best we can do is hope to catch them in a cross fire."

Suddenly, the panic left Dave's face. He nodded once and ran to his horse. As soon as he saw where Barkley was headed, he pointed his horse in the other direction and snapped the reins.

Barkley made it onto his horse, but was hampered by the fresh wound that had ripped through his shoulder. Placing one hand on the wound, he found a bloody gash that was dangerously close to his neck. If that first bullet had clipped him any closer, Barkley knew he would have been in a whole lot of trouble. As it was, he felt more anger than pain.

A few more shots were fired by the riders, but the two groups seemed to be turning in their saddles and trying to figure out how they should approach the separated Rangers. Although the confusion among these men seemed promising at first, Barkley swore under his breath when he saw one of the riders break off and head straight for the charred shed.

Barkley would have liked to keep all of these riders in his sight, but he had some bigger fish to fry before he could do that.

FOURTEEN

Dave dug his heels into his horse's sides and snapped the reins for good measure. Even though he could tell the horse was pouring everything it had into its legs, he wouldn't have minded just a little bit more. He eased up on the animal when he realized that an extra bit of speed wasn't going to help him dodge bullets.

And the bullets were once again starting to fly.

Lead hissed through the air around Dave on either side. As he rode around the riders, they drew closer to him. They were all still moving too quickly to take accurate shots, but each round of gunfire was coming closer to him than the last. Now that he was in the spot Barkley had told him to go and his horse's nose was pointed in the right direction, there was only one thing left for Dave to do.

He shot back at whoever the hell those riders were.

Dave had had plenty of practice in riding and firing at the same time. With a place as big and wide as Texas as their stomping ground, the Rangers found themselves in plenty of chases through open country. Doing his best to ignore the hiss of lead passing by, Dave fired one shot after another.

The smaller group of riders was headed straight for him. They were hunkered down low over their horses' necks and taking their time to aim. They were also riding in crooked lines as opposed to Dave's path. Soon, they made the move that Dave had been dreading and split apart one more time to try and flank him.

Dave shifted in his saddle to take aim at the rider to his right. He pulled his trigger and was shocked to see the rider on the left flop backward and fall from his saddle. Just to be certain, Dave looked down to check if the gun in his hands was bent.

"Hey there," Clint said as he rode up next to Dave with the smoking Colt in his hand. "Looks like you needed some help."

"There's more of them going after Barkley," Dave said.

Clint nodded. "We saw them. Henry went that way."

"And there's another one that went to the shed."

"One thing at a time," Clint said. When he faced forward once again, he didn't have to wait long before another gun was lending its voice to the modified Colt in his own hand.

Clint knew he'd either nicked the second rider or gotten damn close to drawing blood because that man was in a panic. He pulled on his reins almost hard enough to break his horse's neck and tore away from the entire fight.

"Let him go," Clint said to Dave. "Ride ahead and see if Henry needs any help. I'm going to the shack."

Dave showed Clint a quick wave and then steered his horse toward the sound of nearby gunshots. He did a fairly good job of circling around the shack and putting himself in a prime spot to blindside the other riders. By the sound of it, that fight wouldn't last much longer.

A few paces away from the shack, Clint swung one leg over Eclipse's back and jumped from the saddle. When his boots hit the ground, his gun was in his hand and ready to fire. All he needed now was a target.

There was another horse outside the shack, but its saddle was empty. Since the place wasn't much more than a charred wooden shell, it wasn't difficult to hear the sounds of someone rooting around inside. Clint approached the largest wall that was still standing, moved carefully to the edge and then hopped around to face whatever was inside the shed.

Only one man was in sight. He was huddled in one corner, burrowing like a rat in the ashes.

"Stand up," Clint ordered.

The man froze with both hands buried in the filth. The splintered remains of a couple chairs where the bodies had been tied were only a few inches from him. If the bodies hadn't been buried already, the man probably wouldn't have even noticed. In fact, he barely seemed to notice that Clint was there.

"I said stand up," Clint barked.

Outside the shack, gunshots were still being fired. Horses were still stomping against the ground and racing in large circles as one group of men tried to get the killing angle on the other. Inside, on the other hand, Clint felt like he was in the proverbial eye of the storm.

The man who squatted in the ashes was breathing so heavily that it seemed he was panting. Although some of the grime and dirt had fallen away from his hands, he seemed content to keep them mostly covered.

"What've you got there?" Clint asked. "Raise your hands so I can get a look for myself."

Those words sparked something in the man. His eyes narrowed into angry slits, and he let out a snarl that wasn't even vaguely human. As he straightened up, his voice sounded more like a man's. His face, however, was twisted into something brutal and ugly.

The man hopped to his feet and bent his body so he could keep one hand in the muck and lift the other toward the holster slung low at his side. He was surprisingly quick. He even managed to get his fingers around the pistol's grip and lift the gun partway from its leather resting spot.

Clint pulled his trigger and felt the modified Colt buck once against his palm. His bullet punched a hole through the man's heart and dropped him in his own tracks. Even as the man fell over, he kept his other hand buried in the ashen rubble.

Clint looked up and through one of the gaps in the broken wall. He couldn't see much, but he couldn't hear much either.

Considering that he'd heard nothing but gunfire not too long ago, that was a good sign. He stepped forward and kept his gun aimed at the fallen man.

The man's eyes were open and staring at nothing, but there was still an intensity in them that put Clint on his guard. With his gun still ready to put another bullet in him, Clint used the tip of one boot to push the man's hand out from under the filth. Grimy fingers were clenched in a fist, but the sparkle of silver and diamonds could still be seen inside that fist.

"I'll be damned," Clint whispered.

FIFTEEN

A few more shots cracked through the air, but they were aimed at the sky rather than at anything with a pulse.

"And don't come back!" Dave shouted after firing once more.

Henry shook his head and looked over to Barkley. "You all right?"

The tracker nodded and dropped his rifle into the boot hanging from his saddle. "I would've been a whole lot worse if you hadn't showed up. Thanks for the hand."

"You seemed like you were holding your own," Henry replied. "And I don't think I've ever seen Dave so fired up."

The younger Ranger grinned and asked, "Should we take off after them?"

"They could have the sense to sit in those trees they rode for and try to ambush us," Barkley said. "But I doubt it. You're up for another go at those assholes?"

"Hell yes!"

"You two go on, then," Henry said. "Seems only fair for you to get a crack at them since they tried to bushwhack you. I'll see what Clint found in that shed."

Barkley gave Henry a quick nod and steered his horse so he could skirt around the cluster of trees where the escaping gunmen had gone. A snap of leather got his horse moving, and Dave wasn't far behind him.

Although the gunmen had gotten a bit of a head start, Henry didn't favor their chances of staying too far ahead of Barkley. Riding toward the charred shed, he kept his gun in hand and his eyes open for any sign of trouble. Since the shed was barely standing, it wasn't difficult for Henry to spot a figure huddled down inside.

The muscles in Henry's gun arm tensed as he prepared for the worst. "That you, Clint?" he shouted.

When he didn't get a response right away, Henry started to raise his pistol.

Finally, a voice replied to the Texas Ranger's question.

"Yeah," Clint said. "It's me."

"What are you doing in there?"

"Come over here and take a look for yourself."

Henry climbed down from his saddle and holstered his gun. The first thing he saw was Clint squatting beside a body with a fresh hole in its chest.

"Did I interrupt something?" Henry asked with a wary grin.

Clint looked up and then held out his hand. "Take a look at this."

Henry didn't know what to think at first, but that ended as soon as he spotted the silver and diamond brooch in Clint's hand. "Good Lord. Where did you find that?"

"I didn't," Clint replied as he looked down at the body. "He did. Dave said he was one of the men who rode up and tried to shoot him and Barkley."

"And this one came in here after this?"

Clint nodded. "Sounded like the others meant to kill your two men or at least distract them for a bit. Maybe draw them away from here so he could come in and dig this up."

Stepping into the shed, Henry took the brooch from Clint and examined it closely. The jewelry was filthy from being buried in ash and dirt, but no amount of dirt could mask the fact that it was worth a bundle. "This must have belonged to whoever lived here." He looked up at the little space that had been occupied by the shed. "You would've thought these folks could afford somewhere better to live."

"Some folks don't need much," Clint said. "I'm no jeweler, but that piece looks kind of old. It was probably a family heirloom."

"And these greasy bastards had to come all this way to loot it." Suddenly, Henry snapped his eyes up and grinned.

"You just remember something funny?" Clint asked.

"Not exactly funny, but I did remember something. As far as I know, nobody spent too much time at the other places that were burnt up. Most of them were out in the open like this and were just left to be knocked down or cleared away by whoever was gonna claim the land."

"Are you sure about that?"

"Whatever happened to those places," Henry explained, "didn't happen until me and my men were long gone. What I mean is that someone could have easily circled back to sift through what was left."

Clint stood up and dusted himself off. "You think these men are the ones you've been after?"

"They could be. There's more than one of them. They're definitely killers, since they tried to kill you as well as me and my boys just now. If they knew about this," he added while holding out the brooch, "then they might have known about stuff the others had."

Looking around at the small square of space enclosed by the four broken walls, Clint winced and shook his head. "I doubt these folks strayed more than a few miles from this place. It sure doesn't seem like they were prominent enough for someone all the way in Texas to know who they were or what possessions they owned."

"Even if they knew about one bunch of family heirlooms like this one, it'd make it more than worth their while to go and round them all up."

Clint scraped at the ground with his boot. The blackened floorboards had been pulled up, and there was only a shallow hole under one of them where the brooch must have been kept. Other than that, there was nothing beneath Clint's boot except for more charred earth. "There wasn't anything else here worth stealing," Clint said solemnly. "And not nearly enough that was worth getting burned alive."

But Henry's enthusiasm wasn't affected. "I could check with another friend of mine who might know if these folks could have known some of the others that were killed," he said.

"You mean another Texas Ranger?" Clint asked.

Now it was Henry's turn to wince. "Not exactly. I doubt the Rangers would be too happy if they knew how far I'd gone from . . ."

"From the Texas border?" Clint asked.

"Yeah. That may be a sticky subject when I get back."

"Not if you come back with the scalps of those killers hanging off your belt."

"True . . . so to speak. Until then, I'd rather not ruffle any feathers that ain't already been ruffled, if you know what I mean."

"Yes," Clint replied. "I know what you mean. Hopefully those friends of yours are close, because I don't think there's a telegraph office anywhere near here."

"They're close. Think you can wait a bit for me until I come back? You've been a real help and I'd hate to lose you too soon just in case this ride ain't over yet."

"I'll head back to Kipperway and see about putting that brooch in the proper hands. After that, I can check in on your boys in the next town over."

Henry nodded and tipped his hat. "I'd appreciate that. Seems like Rick Hartman wasn't lying when he mentioned what an asset you were in a bad situation."

"I'd only believe half of what Rick says," Clint replied. "Fortunately for you, what he told you falls into the good half."

SIXTEEN

It seemed like a full day since Clint had left the Kipperway Tavern. When he walked back into it, he looked as if he'd gone through a war. His face was dirty from the ashes and soot that had been kicked up at the shack. His clothes were filthy with more of the same as well as a good amount of trail dust. Even his eyes seemed bleary.

As he walked up to the bar, Clint was surprised that nobody seemed to pay him any mind. He thought it was possible that he felt worse than he looked. Then again, it was never wise to underestimate just how wrapped up most folks were in themselves.

"Holy crow," the Irish barkeep said. "You look like you need a drink."

"Thanks for noticing," Clint said. "One of those fine beers would go a long way."

"Actually, it looks like something a bit stronger is in order." Before Clint could protest, the barkeep slapped a small glass onto the bar and poured two fingers of whiskey into it. "There you go. Cuts through the dust better than anything else I know."

Even though Clint wasn't much of a whiskey drinker, what he'd seen in the last several hours had left a mighty bad taste in his mouth. He picked up the whiskey glass and tossed it back. The liquor still wasn't his favorite, but its taste was a whole lot better than the gritty ash that had settled in the back of his throat. The warm jolt from the alcohol even seemed to stoke some of the fire that had been sputtering in his belly.

"Not bad, huh?" the barkeep asked.

"Not bad, but I'll stick to beer," Clint replied. "I'll also need a room for the night."

Turning around to the wall behind him, the barkeep said, "I've got one or two of those that aren't spoken for. And . . . um . . . if I may suggest a bath?"

"Normally I might take offense to that," Clint said. "But under the circumstances . . ."

"Give me the word and I'll have the water sent up. You're in room number three."

Clint took the key that was handed over to him as well as the mug of beer that was placed onto the bar. "The word's given. Just point me toward the stairs."

"No stairs," the barkeep replied. "But the rooms are right over that way."

Clint looked in the direction the barkeep was pointing. At first, all he saw was the small stage where a couple of dancing girls were kicking up their skirts. Then he caught sight of a small door with the word "ROOMS" painted on it in dark red letters.

"Good enough for me," Clint said. "I'll be expecting my bathwater."

"I'm sure you won't have to wait very long."

Making his way through the saloon, Clint didn't spot any familiar faces or even anyone who took much notice of him. Apparently, filthy men with saddlebags slung over one shoulder weren't uncommon in the place. When he got to the door, Clint was dismayed to find it locked.

"Damn," he muttered.

Before he got too upset, Clint checked his hand and found two keys instead of just one. The fact that he'd missed the second key on the ring told Clint how tired he was. Either way, he was just glad one of the keys fit into the lock on the door and the second key opened room number three.

As far as rented rooms in the back of a saloon go, Clint's was fairly nice. It was clean and had fresh linens on the bed, which was already several steps above the typical rooms to be found so close to a bar. He chuckled to himself when he saw that the oddly shaped table against the wall was actually an overturned bathtub that had been mostly covered up by a small tablecloth.

By the time Clint removed the tablecloth and flipped the bathtub over, he heard a knock on his door.

Since he was currently trapped between the tub and the wall, Clint shouted, "Come in."

There was some fidgeting at the door before it was finally pushed open by someone's foot. Clint was very pleased to see that the foot was attached to a shapely leg.

"Think you could give me a hand with these?" Belle asked as she took a shuffling step inside while carrying a bucket in each hand.

Clint moved around the tub and rushed over to take both of the buckets from her. "I thought you might work here, but I didn't think you were hired to carry water."

"I wasn't hired to carry water," she replied breathlessly. "And I wasn't hired for what you may have been thinking, either. I deal faro."

Laughing nervously, Clint said, "I wasn't going to suggest otherwise. I thought you might have served drinks or something." Lifting up one of the buckets, he tipped it to pour the water into the tub. "Maybe you got up on the stage from time to time."

Belle stood beside him and emptied the other bucket into the tub. "I do get up there sometimes, but only when one of the regular girls ain't feeling too well."

"So why the special treatment?" Clint asked.

Smiling and averting her eyes a bit, she said, "I never got a chance to thank you properly for stepping in earlier."

After all that had happened recently, Clint had to take a moment and think about what she was talking about.

"Stepping in with Red, I mean," Belle explained after she saw Clint floundering for a bit.

"Sorry. It's been a long day."

"Don't worry about it. I'll get the rest of the water."

Clint walked along with her to carry in four of the next six bucket loads. Once the tub was full with steaming water, Belle shut the door and walked across the room to where Clint was standing.

"I was going to take my bath before the water gets cold," Clint said.

"Wrong," Belle announced as she unbuttoned Clint's shirt. "We're taking that bath."

SEVENTEEN

Clint unbuckled his gun belt and draped it over a chair while Belle stripped off his shirt. Her hands never left his body, and she slid her fingertips along his bare chest while lowering herself onto her knees in front of him. She looked up at him while she opened his pants and slipped her hand inside.

"Thank you," she whispered as she took his penis in her hand and began stroking it.

"You're welcome," Clint replied. When he saw her stand up and slide her dress down off her shoulders, he added, "You're very, very welcome."

Belle smiled and lowered her head to look down at her pert, rounded breasts. Her nipples were the size of dimes and were already getting hard. As she worked her dress the rest of the way down, she wiggled her hips slowly until the garment fell into a pile around her feet. She then stepped out of it and walked slowly toward the tub.

"Let's not let this water get cold," she said.

Clint eagerly finished getting undressed and stepped into the tub. The water was a bit too hot at first, but it did a nice job of making everything else seem to melt away. Everything else, that is, except for Belle.

The moment he rested his shoulders against the tub, Clint felt Belle's hands massaging his tired muscles. Almost immediately, he closed his eyes and let out a slow, contented sigh.

"You like that?" she asked.

"Oh yeah."

Belle slipped her hand down along Clint's chest and leaned forward so she could reach between his legs. "How about now?"

She couldn't quite reach as far down as Clint would have liked, but Belle seemed content to tease him by stopping just short of stroking him again.

"Could be better," Clint said with a grin.

"Really? We'll just have to see about that."

Taking a sponge in one hand and some soap in the other, Belle scrubbed Clint from head to toe. She circled the tub and ran her hands along the slippery surface of his skin while spreading the soap all the way around. After stepping to the side of the tub, Belle was able to reach all the way beneath the water and massage Clint's growing erection. As she continued to work her hand along Clint's shaft, she leaned over to kiss him on the lips.

The kiss started off good enough, but soon it curled Clint's toes. As she slipped her tongue into his mouth, she pumped her hand faster on his cock. Before too long, Clint was reaching out of the tub to pull her closer.

"Oh no you don't," Belle said as she pulled away from him. "I'm not getting into that filthy water with you."

"After that kiss, you're either coming in here or I'm climbing out of here and going after you."

Belle smiled mischievously and turned her back to Clint. Walking naked across the floor, she moved toward the bed and shifted her hips like a cat stalking its prey. "I suppose I couldn't stop you if you wanted to come after me," she said over her shoulder.

Clint was up and out of the tub in a heartbeat. His wet feet skidded on the floor, but he somehow managed to get to the bed without falling and breaking his neck. By the time he got to her, Clint and Belle were both laughing.

Taking her into his arms, Clint kissed her long and hard on her soft lips. Her firm breasts were pressed against his chest and one of her legs was draped over him. They both lay on their sides, but soon Clint was positioning himself on top of her.

He took one of her hands in his as he slipped his other hand around to cup her tight backside. His cock rubbed against the moist lips between her legs. Soon, he could feel Belle using her free hand to guide him into her. As Clint pushed his hips forward, he could feel Belle pulling in an anxious breath. He kept still for a moment, until she was trembling with anticipation, and then finally drove all the way into her.

Belle gripped him tightly and arched her back against the bed. She spread her legs open wide and clenched her eyes shut as Clint started to pound into her with growing intensity. Soon, a pleasured moan built up in the back of her throat and was slowly pushed past her lips.

Sliding his hand from Belle's wrist and down her arm, Clint savored the touch of her smooth skin as he continued pumping in and out of her. After running his palm over her hip, he reached around to cup her buttocks in both hands. From there, he thrust his hips powerfully enough to make Belle's entire body shake.

"Oh God," she moaned. "Oh God, yes."

Clint positioned himself so he was on his knees between her legs. He kept thrusting in and out of her while moving both of his hands over her belly. He could feel her straining her muscles to keep from screaming even louder. That control was put to the test even more when he held both of her breasts and kneaded them as he entered her with slower, stronger strokes.

Belle breathed in short, passionate gasps. Her head was tossed to one side, and she grabbed onto the mattress in a strong grip. As her climax rushed in to take her over, she grabbed hold of Clint's hips and moved them faster and harder. Never one to deny a lady what she wanted, Clint made his thrusts faster and harder.

Pumping her own hips in time to Clint's, Belle rubbed against his rigid cock until she was overpowered by her climax. When she finally let out the breath that had caught in her throat, it was with a slow, satisfied groan.

She opened her eyes and looked at Clint with a grin. Once again, Belle started pumping her hips, but she was doing it more to put a smile onto Clint's face. When she saw him looking down at her, she began to rub her fingertips along his chest and nibble on the side of his neck.

Clint was only human, and it didn't take much more of that before he exploded inside of her. Belle wrapped her legs around him and ground her body against him until he was barely strong enough to keep from falling over. It took all the strength he had left to lower himself onto his side next to Belle.

"Oh my," Belle said with a giggle. "After that, I feel like I need to thank you again."

"Sure," Clint replied breathlessly. "Just give me a minute to catch my breath."

EIGHTEEN

By the time Clint got up from his bed, it was late enough for the saloon to have quieted down, but early enough for the first rays of sunlight to seep through his window. Belle had kept him so busy that his legs were weak and his muscles ached. Even so, it was the kind of fatigue that he would take any day of the year.

The beer he'd brought to the room had been sitting around for way too long, but Clint took a drink of it anyway. When he lowered the mug, he wore a vaguely surprised look on his face.

"Well, what did you expect?" Belle asked. "That beer's been sitting there long enough to dry up."

"That's not what surprised me," Clint said. "It's actually still pretty damn good."

Belle extended her hand and motioned for Clint to pass it. He handed the beer over so she could take a sip. Apparently, she wasn't as impressed, because she almost immediately handed it back. "Maybe I should get dressed and fetch us something better to drink," she offered.

Perfectly content to sip his stale beer, Clint sat back and watched Belle get dressed. It wasn't long before she realized she was being watched and shifted her movements accordingly. Her hips swayed a bit more than normal, and she leaned forward for a bit longer than if she'd been on her own.

"Are you going to tell me what happened when you charged out of here?" she asked as she slowly buttoned her stockings to her garter belt.

"I got a hunch that that friend of yours was going to make a move on that shed sooner rather than later."

"You mean Red?"

Clint nodded. "He seemed pretty interested in that place when we had our conversation in the street."

"Why?"

Although Clint pulled on some of his clothes, he didn't reach in to take the brooch from where he'd stashed it. Instead, he asked her, "Do you know of anyone else who might be friends or family of the folks that lived there?"

"Not as such. I only lived near the Wilkins place," she explained. "They didn't really say much to me."

"Well, it seemed they had a few valuable pieces of jewelry that Red was after."

"Is that a fact?"

"Yep. You sure you don't know of anyone who might have proper rights to something like that?"

She thought about it a bit more, but Belle had to reluctantly shake her head. "I hardly ever saw them leave that place of theirs and I never saw anyone else go in. Sorry."

"It's all right. Thanks for your help, though."

Belle left the room and wasn't gone for very long before returning. Clint had just enough time to get dressed and make certain the brooch was safe and sound in one of his pockets.

Before she opened the door again, Belle knocked. She peeked inside as if hoping to catch Clint in a compromising situation. When she found him sitting on the edge of the bed fully dressed, she shrugged and came inside anyway.

"Here you go," she said while handing over a cup of water. "I didn't know if you wanted another beer."

"This'll be fine," Clint replied.

As he drank the cool water, Clint saw Belle snap her fingers and twist around to face him.

"I just remembered something!" she said anxiously.

"What?"

"It was something I wanted to tell you before you flew out of here in such a rush the last time. Do you remember that?"

"Not exactly, but go ahead."

Belle furrowed her brow and fixed him with a stern look.

"All right, I remember," Clint lied. "What did you want to tell me?"

"There was another fire."

The smirk that had been on Clint's face instantly disappeared. "What was that?" he asked.

"It was in Solace. That's the town a little ways west of here. I hope it wasn't too bad."

Plenty of fires were sparked that had more to do with dry lumber and carelessness than any sort of malicious intent. Even so, Clint couldn't help but feel that he was about to get one of his worst suspicions confirmed.

There was only one way for him to be certain.

NINETEEN

"I'm going to Solace," Clint said.

Henry sat in the restaurant inside the hotel where he was staying and stared across his table at Clint. He kept staring at him, as if he was waiting for the punch line to a joke. Finally, he asked, "What are you talking about?"

"Solace," Clint repeated. "It's the name of the town where Bower went. I heard there was another fire over there."

"Was anyone killed?"

"I don't know yet."

"Then maybe it doesn't have anything to do with why we're here," Henry said.

Speaking through a mouthful of eggs and potatoes, Talman grunted, "Fires spark up all the time. It don't mean every last one of 'em was sparked by a killer."

"I know that," Clint said evenly. "But this just seems like an awfully big coincidence. I don't like coincidences."

"Like 'em or not, they tend to happen," Talman snapped.

Clint threw half a glance at Talman, but kept his eyes mostly on Henry. Eventually, the leader of the Texas Rangers wiped off his mouth and slapped his napkin down.

"We've still got work to do here," Henry said. "Barkley and Dave have to check in and we can't just leave 'em high and dry. Besides, Bower and Mark are in that town."

"And have they checked in?" Clint asked.

"No."

"Maybe that means something."

"Or maybe you're talking out of your ass," Talman muttered.

This time, Clint put more than half a stare on Talman. He placed his hands flat upon the Rangers' table and leaned down like a wolf preparing to rip a smaller animal's head off.

"What the hell even got you to come along on this hunt, Talman?" Clint asked. "Was there a pay increase or were you just looking to get out of some other work in Texas that needed to be done?"

Talman jumped up from his chair and nearly overturned the table along the way. Before he could say anything, he was being shoved back down again by the man next to him.

"We wanted to keep from drawing too much attention here, gentlemen," Henry warned. "This ain't exactly the best way to go about it."

Talman choked back whatever it was he'd wanted to say and nodded slowly. He also made a point to try to look like he was sitting back down again on his own accord.

"Those men we traded shots with are still out there," Henry said to Clint. "They're the closest we've gotten to catching someone at the spot of one of these fires and I ain't about to let them get away."

"What if they're not the ones you're after?" Clint asked.

"Then they need to learn not to shoot at a Texas Ranger. They fired on a lawman, Adams. You know I can't just let them ride away after that."

"All right," Clint said. "That's fair enough. I wasn't even here to ask if you'd come along with me. I'm going to Solace to see what's going on over there. I just thought you'd like to know."

Talman let out a clipped grunt of a laugh before saying, "That was a good way to waste some time."

Before Clint could respond to that, Henry shifted in his seat to glare at his partner. "I swear to Christ you're more trouble than you're worth, Talman. If you don't stop making an ass out of yourself, you will become a bigger pain in my ass than I'm willing to bear. After that, you might as well get on your horse and keep riding north because you won't want to step foot in Texas again."

Although Henry's voice wasn't loud enough to carry much past their table, there was more than enough intensity in it to tell Clint he was serious. Apparently, Talman knew that just as well.

Like a child who'd been freshly scolded, Talman looked down and picked at his food without saying another word.

Once he saw that he'd put an end to one source of his headache, Henry shifted his attention back to the other. "You want to go see what's happening in Solace?" Henry asked. "Go on ahead. I appreciate all the help you're giving me, Clint, but you don't take orders from me. You can go do whatever you like. All I ask is that you find a way to get word to me if you happen to find something that may be of some use. If you're not willing to do that, I can't back you up if this situation gets any worse."

Clint shook his head. "I wouldn't expect you to back me up unless I was helping you. If I do find something over there, I'll be sure you find out about it."

"All right, then," Henry said. "Since you're going all that way to check on my boys, maybe you should take this along with you."

When Clint saw what Henry was handing over to him, he instantly knew why the Texas Ranger had been so hard on him. The badge was in somewhat rougher shape when compared to the ones worn by Henry, Talman and the others, but it still looked official enough.

"I don't know how much weight that'll carry around these parts," Henry said, "but it could cut a few conversations short if you need to speed things up with a local authority."

Clint's first impulse was to hand the badge back to Henry. Still, despite being out of Texas, the Rangers had a good enough reputation to get plenty of things done plenty of other places. Seeing as how there might still be a killer on the loose, Clint decided not to turn his nose up at whatever help was being offered.

"I'll make sure to keep my nose clean," Clint said as he tucked the badge into his pocket.

"Be sure that you do," Henry warned. "Or I'll just have to come after you as soon as I've got this other killer's hide tacked onto the side of my barn."

TWENTY

When he got back to his room at the Kipperway Tavern, Clint found Belle lying in his bed wearing nothing but her stockings and a smile. She flipped the sheets off the bed, inviting him to lie beside her without having to say a word.

"This is the hardest thing I've ever had to do," Clint said. "But I've got to leave."

"What?" Belle asked with a stunned expression on her face. "Why?"

"I need to go to Solace, but I'll be back before too long."

Even though he'd been the one to take the smile off her face, Clint could hardly bear the sight of her pulling the sheets up around her and moving off the bed.

"You truly can't know how difficult this is," Clint said.

Belle walked up to him, looked Clint in the eyes and slipped her hand between his legs. Feeling the bulge in his crotch grow harder after a bit of coaxing, she grinned and said, "I can tell how hard it is."

"That's not fair, Belle. It really isn't."

"Now we both feel slighted. Do you want to know how I feel?"

Without waiting for an answer, she took Clint's hand and guided it between her own legs. She was warm, soft and wet enough to make the pain Clint felt before seem like nothing in comparison to the aching he felt now.

Clint bit down on his lower lip.

"You still want to go?" she purred.

After letting out a strained breath, Clint said, "Yes. It's important."

She examined him for a few more seconds before stepping back and picking up her clothes. "I suppose it must be pretty important. Either that, or I'm losing my touch."

"You're not losing anything," Clint said. "I just hope you'll be here when I get back."

"Maybe not right in this room, but I'll be around. When you get back here, come find me and I'll let you convince me to give you another chance."

"I'll look forward to it."

Belle was merciful enough to get dressed quickly and pat his cheek as she walked toward the door. "Don't stay away too long, now."

Clint needed a moment to stand in his room once Belle was gone. He collected himself, gathered some breath and let it out. Suddenly, he felt very tired. Before he gave in to that feeling, he packed up his saddlebag, slung it over his shoulder and headed out.

While he was getting Eclipse ready to go, Clint spotted something down the street that held his attention. He quickly finished up what he was doing and made certain every one of the saddle's buckles and straps were tightly fastened. Taking the reins in hand, Clint led Eclipse down the street to the small building that had caught his eye.

The little church wasn't very fancy. The bell it its little tower looked as if it hadn't been rung in years. The door was warped and the windows were cracked, but the old preacher who tended to them did so as if he was maintaining the finest cathedral in the country.

As Clint walked up to the preacher, he smiled and thought back to just how long it had been since he'd been to a proper service.

"Good morning, friend," the preacher said. He was an old Mexican with stringy white hair and a round, pleasant face.

"There won't be a mass until noon, but you're welcome to stay and pass some time in the shade."

"No, thanks, Father. Is that the proper title?"

The preacher chuckled and waved his hand dismissively. "I've been called worse. What can I do for you?"

"Do you know about the folks who died in that fire the other day?"

"Oh yes," the preacher replied as a shadow seemed to settle on his face. "Today's mass is in their honor."

"Did they have any family?"

"I'm not sure, but if they do, they'll probably be at the mass. You're welcome to attend as well."

Clint shook his head and dug into his pocket. "I can't attend, Father, but I would like to give you this. It belonged to . . . the departed."

Holding out his hand, the preacher gasped when he saw the brooch that was placed onto his palm. "Oh my goodness! This belonged to Maryanne Wilkins?"

At that moment, Clint didn't know what made him feel worse: the fact that he didn't know the dead woman's name or the fact that he was prepared to lie to the preacher about that fact. Finally, Clint bit the bullet and replied, "I didn't know them, but I found it in their house. It's a long story and it's not as bad as it sounds. Just . . . please see to it that it's given to the proper person."

"Certainly. If there's a next of kin, I'll be sure to pass it on."

"I'd appreciate it, Father."

Just then, the preacher lifted his chin and showed Clint a warm smile. He even started to nod slowly, as if he was listening to someone else's voice. "May the Lord bless you, sir."

It took a moment, but Clint asked, "What's that for?"

"Because I can tell you truly would appreciate it if this finds its proper owner. So many would keep such a treasure for themselves and not think twice about it."

"Yeah, I suppose they would."

Still smiling, the preacher extended his arm and made the sign of the cross over Clint's forehead.

"Oh, and Father?" Clint asked once the blessing was done. "It's probably best if you don't let folks know you have that until you're sure there is a proper heir."

The preacher chuckled and said, "I may be a man of peace, but I'm no stranger to the black sheep in my flock."

TWENTY-ONE

The old barn had stood in its spot for years. Most locals would say it had been there longer than the rest of the town of Solace. It was a big old building that had become home to plenty of animals other than the ones brought in by the farmer who'd owned the place.

That farmer was gone.

He'd been gone for quite a while, allowing the animals to take the barn over. A few of the original residents may have had some offspring that still remained, but most of the animal life in that place had been of the wild variety.

Coyotes, jackrabbits and even a few strains of birds made their home there. At least, it had been their home before Voorhees had come along to burn it to the ground.

Voorhees stood in his spot and pulled in a long breath filled with soot and the stench of death. Those things brought a smile to his face and a wistful sigh all the way up from the back of his throat.

When he heard footsteps approaching him, he was reluctant to shift his eyes away from the smoking frame of the barn. When he saw who was walking up to stand beside him, he shifted his eyes back and licked the smoky grit from his teeth.

"What's the meaning of this?" Elizabeth asked.

Voorhees dug his hands into his pockets and spoke through clenched teeth. "It was a fire. A big one."

"Why didn't you tell me about this? You're not supposed to do something like this unless I tell you to."

"There were so many inside. I couldn't wait."

Stepping around to stand in front of him, Elizabeth glared up at the tall man's lumpy face. "How many were in there?"

"I don't know."

Elizabeth slapped him hard enough to make a loud crack, but that was still not enough to turn his head more than a fraction of an inch. "How many?" she demanded.

"Lots," Voorhees replied as he reached up with one hand to lovingly rub the spot where he'd been slapped.

Looking around at the overgrown field and rocky soil, Elizabeth asked, "Do you even know if anyone saw the fire?"

"No."

As much as she wanted to slap him again, Elizabeth held back. The last thing she wanted to do was make the moment better for Voorhees. "I've got a plan for another fire," she explained as calmly as she could manage. "We may be able to get a whole street this time."

Voorhees's eyes widened and his mouth hung open. "A whole street?"

"That's right. But we won't be able to do that if you go around doing things like this and put folks on their guard. I think some of those lawmen are here."

"The Texas Rangers?"

She nodded. "The Texas Rangers. They want to catch us real bad, and they might just get us if we stay in one place too long or if we get too sloppy."

Slowly, Voorhees hung his head. "Sorry."

Elizabeth extended a tightly clenched fist up to his face. Through a great amount of effort, she uncurled her fingers and rubbed Voorhees's chin. "Why would you do this without me? You know I like to be here when they die. And afterward, I like to be with you."

"I know, but there were so many and I didn't want them to run away."

Looking toward the tall, blackened posts that had supported

one of the barn's crumbled walls, Elizabeth asked, "Was it good?"

Voorhees nodded slowly, as though he was fondly remembering a childhood dream. "It was real good. They were howling and screaming and kicking at the walls. Some of them tried to fly out, but their wings were on fire."

"Fly out?"

He kept nodding. "Some of them had nests in the loft."

"Are you talking about birds?"

"Yes. They were the best. But some of the others inside screamed louder. I went to try and see what they were, but there was too much smoke. All I could see was them running and dragging themselves."

"Were there any people inside?" Elizabeth asked.

"I don't think so. If there were, they were real quiet."

Elizabeth smiled and patted his cheek. "Then maybe this isn't so bad after all. Nobody may even remember this place is here."

"I'll remember it. Just like I remember all the others."

"I know, darling. I know."

Voorhees tilted his head, but didn't quite put his face into Elizabeth's hands. When he looked toward the barn, he made a noise that was something close to a purr.

"I want to go inside and look," he said.

"If you want, you can stay here overnight."

"Really?"

"Yes. That will give me some time to take another look around and find the best spots for you to burn. Those streets I saw are perfect and they should burn so good."

"What if those lawmen find me?" Voorhees asked.

Elizabeth's reply was short and sweet. "Then you'll kill them. If they insist on chasing us this far, they'll have to be dealt with."

"Do you think a Texas Ranger will scream when he's on fire?"

Now Elizabeth smiled fondly. "Yes, darling. I think he will."

TWENTY-TWO

Compared to Kipperway, Solace was the cosmopolitan center of New Mexico. There were several streets leading into different sections of town, ranging from a row of well-maintained shops to a brightly decorated Chinatown district. Not every stretch of street was up to the standards held by the majority, but those exceptions were on the edge of town and were most likely occupied by cheap saloons and rat-infested cathouses.

As Clint rode down the streets looking for the Archer Hotel, he took some comfort in the fact that he was less likely to be noticed riding into a town this size. Unlike Kipperway, the locals here didn't pay any mind to a strange face in the street. When he spotted a particular storefront on the corner, Clint thought he might have found the exception to that rule.

According to the sign over the door, the *Solace Examiner* was New Mexico's finest source of reputable information. As Clint dismounted and tied Eclipse's reins to a hitching post, he hoped that whoever ran the newspaper would at least know something about any fires started in the last few days.

The narrow door leading into the newspaper office was closed, but not locked. When Clint opened it, he was immediately assaulted by the smells of ink, wood pulp and axle grease. Judging by the look of the man who poked his head up from behind one of the presses, Clint realized that those smells were the least of his worries.

"Can I help you?" the man asked. His face was smeared with dark grease and his hair was slicked down by it. Even so, he smirked at Clint and even showed him a friendly wave. "I'm open for business, if you're out to place an advertisement or the like."

"Not exactly," Clint said. Since he didn't want to be rude, he shook the man's hand and got his own smeared in the mess covering the other fellow. "I wanted to ask about some fires here recently."

"There's been another one? Just a moment and I'll get my pencil."

Before the man could get out from where he was entrenched behind the machines, Clint said, "I don't know about another one here, but there has been one in Kipperway."

"The one at the Wilkins place?"

"That's the one."

"I already printed a story about it. Actually, I was running off that very copy when my press jammed up. You wouldn't happen to know how to fix one of these, would you?"

Clint looked down at the press and shrugged. "I may if you could let me know about some of the other newsworthy events that have been going on around here."

"Don't you read the *Examiner*?"

"I'm not from around here, and I don't have the time to catch up right now. That's why it would be a big help if you could tell me about the fire that was started here recently."

The newspaperman grinned and wiped the sweat from his brow. "Ah, now I see. You want to hear about it before it's printed, eh? To be honest, I didn't think folks cared so much about what I print that they'd want to get a jump on it."

"You'd be saving me some time."

"Well, you mentioned you could help me out with my little situation here?"

Clint took a few steps forward and fixed his eyes upon the newspaperman as if he was bargaining for his life. He then extended one leg and used his boot to knock out a chunk of broken wood from where it had been wedged into the machinery. Clint may not have been an expert in how a press worked, but he knew this one would work a whole lot better once that hunk of wood was removed.

Jumping at the way the press creaked and settled back into its normal positioning, the newspaperman leaned forward to see what Clint had done. When he saw the chunk of wood on the floor, he grinned and shook his head. "I knew I'd lost a piece of that crate."

"Now, about those fires."

"I suppose it's fair enough that I tell you. Of course, you could have just taken a look at the copies I'd printed out already."

When Clint looked over to where the newspaperman was pointing, he saw a short stack of papers next to the machine.

"Not that it's any big secret," the man continued. "I'm going to have to apologize in advance for the disappointing nature of the news you worked so hard to hear."

"Try me," Clint replied. "I didn't really work that hard."

"There was a fire here recently, but it was just a barn that burned down. Actually," the newspaperman added as he walked around the press and wiped his hands on the heavy apron he wore, "it was an abandoned old barn a little ways outside of town. The only real surprise was that it hadn't burned down long ago. Sorry to build it up so much."

But Clint was far from disappointed. In fact, he was quite relieved to hear the news, as opposed to hearing that more folks had been killed before he'd gotten into town. "No problem. You've got to do your part to try to sell your papers."

"Spoken like a true kindred spirit. Have you worked among the ink and paper?"

"No."

"Would you like to?"

"Tell you what," Clint said as he walked toward the door. "If I do need work while I'm in town, this is the first place I'll visit."

The newspaperman seemed pleased with that and said, "My name's Eldon Slattery. Who might you be?"

Although Eldon seemed like a nice enough sort, Clint

thought twice about letting the town's reporter know his name. Having the Gunsmith show up in the next edition wasn't the best way to keep his head down.

"I'm Clint," he replied curtly. "Now, if you'll excuse me, I must be going."

Clint's short reply was enough for Eldon, who flipped one hand as if he was tipping an invisible hat. "Thanks for the hand, Clint. Or rather, the boot."

"No problem, Eldon. Thanks for the good news. You know where I can find the Archer Hotel?"

TWENTY-THREE

Clint knocked on the door of the room that had been rented by the two Texas Rangers. He stood outside and calmly waited for the door to open. When it did and Bower looked outside, the expression on his face made the buildup more than worth it.

"What in the hell are you doing here?" the young Ranger asked.

"Well, hello to you, too," Clint replied. "Mind if I come in?"

Obviously more worried about carrying out Henry's order to stay unnoticed, Bower checked the hallway before opening the door all the way and motioning for Clint to step through. He waited until the door was shut again before saying, "Now tell me what you're doing here. Did Henry send you?"

"Yeah. We had a scrap with a bunch of gunmen looking to loot what was left of that house."

"The house that was burned?"

"That's the one."

Bower thought that over, but still seemed just as confused. "What was left to rob?"

"Some jewelry. Pretty nice stuff, too."

"Damn," Bower muttered. "I wonder if all them other places were robbed."

"You see there?" Clint asked with a smirk. "You've already thought farther ahead than your friend Talman."

Bower let out a grunting breath. "He ain't my friend. That man's an ass."

"I knew I liked you, kid," Clint said. "Did you know about the fire at that barn?"

"Did you?"

Clint nodded, but kept his source to himself for the moment. Once again, the startled expression on Bower's face made it worth the effort.

"Yeah," Bower said. "I knew about it. From what we can tell, it was just an old barn. It doesn't sound like anyone was hurt."

"Are you certain about that?"

"We will be before too long. Mark rode out there to get a look for himself to see if there are any . . . bodies."

Considering how many deaths the group of Texas Rangers had seen lately, it seemed a bit odd to hear one of them sound squeamish at the mention of another one. Then again, being callous to such matters wasn't exactly a good thing.

"Sounds like you've got things well in hand," Clint pointed out.

Bower nodded and asked, "What about things in Kipperway? I heard there was some trouble there, but I didn't know you traded shots with anyone."

Clint looked at the younger man's face and saw hopeful expectation in his eyes. As much as he didn't want to chip away at Henry's authority, Clint also thought the kid should know what kind of man he was riding with where Talman was concerned. Finally, once Clint realized he was about to speak from his own aggravation, he told the Texas Ranger the truth.

"All things considered, things over there are going pretty well," Clint stated.

"Good. I'm just surprised Talman hasn't bagged those assholes yet."

Clint thought he deserved a medal for keeping his mouth shut after that one.

"Now that there's two of us here, maybe we should go

after Mark," Bower said. "I was thinking that I shouldn't go anywhere before he came back, but he's been gone awhile."

"I wouldn't worry too much about him," Clint said. "From what I hear, that barn's been deserted for a good long time."

"How'd you come by that information?"

"I've got my sources," Clint said cryptically. "When was Mark supposed to meet you?"

"Over an hour ago."

"And how far away is that barn?"

"A mile or so."

Although Clint had been feeling confident before, those words brought him right back down to Bower's level. "And how long's he been gone so far?"

"A few hours," Bower replied.

"Do you know the route he was taking to get to that barn?" Clint asked.

The younger man nodded.

"Good," Clint said. "Tell it to me and I'll follow it to see if I can find him. You wait here in case he gets past me and comes back."

"Maybe I should be the one to go to that barn."

"Nah," Clint said as confidently as he could manage. "I'll go." Since that was the best he could manage on such short notice, Clint headed for the door and walked out before Bower had much of a chance to say anything about it.

"Which way do I go from here?" Clint asked as he started shutting the door behind him.

Bower hesitated for a moment, but the next words he spoke were the directions Clint was after. "There's an alley across the street from this hotel. Cut through it and cut through the next few alleys until you're headed out of town. But I still think I might—"

Just to put the younger man's second thoughts to rest, Clint added, "All right. You check those alleys to see if Mark's there, but I'll head to the barn. That way, we can keep out of sight just the way Henry wanted. If I'm not back before too long, make sure your guns are loaded and come after me."

If Bower had any other misgivings, Clint didn't stay around long enough to hear them. If those killers were nearby, Clint wasn't about to put anyone else in jeopardy by waiting one more second before going after them.

TWENTY-FOUR

Clint followed the directions he'd been given and wound up with a quick tour of Solace. The shortcut through the alleys would have led him straight through the heart of the town and pointed him in the right direction once he was out of it. Following that same basic path but using the normal streets, Clint rode out of town and down the narrow trail leading to the properties surrounding it.

Thankfully, the land was fairly flat and the only growth was a few scrub bushes and the occasional rock. Clint wasn't much of a farmer, but he was getting a real good idea of why a barn might be abandoned in such a place. And with so many cattle barons in the surrounding areas, a small ranch would have even more trouble prospering.

Before he could think too long about who'd built the barn in the first place, Clint could see the old structure ahead. There was a broken fence surrounding a small patch of ground, leading Clint to believe the previous owners may have raised pigs or even a few horses. By the looks of it now, the spread was only good for collecting dust.

The barn was a blackened hulk, reminding Clint of the shack that he'd been shown in the next town over. While this place was bigger, it was still a charred shadow of what it had been before. It truly looked like a collection of walls and floorboards had been killed to leave behind an empty husk.

Plenty of places burned down. Some places caught fire more than once, but this single place in the middle of nowhere struck a chord in Clint's mind. The similarities could have been in his head, but his first guess was that the flames hadn't just shown up by accident.

"Mark?" Clint shouted as he reined Eclipse to a stop. "Are you here?"

Not only was there no reply, but there were no sounds whatsoever drifting through the air. For a place stuck in the middle of critter-infested land, that was no small feat.

As Clint climbed down from his saddle and walked toward the barn, he could smell something else that struck a chord in him. It was a bitter taint to the expected scents of burned wood and smoke that told him something had died in those flames.

Clint's hand came to a rest on his holstered Colt and the muscles in his arm reflexively prepared to draw.

"Mark? It's Clint Adams. Can you hear me?"

Although he didn't get a proper response, Clint did hear something inside the barn move. The noise caught his ear, but that wasn't anything too extraordinary considering the condition of the place. The rustling that he'd heard could have been anything inside the blackened corpse of a building falling down or giving way. Even so, Clint steeled himself and walked toward the barn.

One of the front barn doors had completely fallen in, and the other had splintered diagonally in half, making the front of the building look like it was wearing a gap-toothed smile. The closer Clint got to the place, the stronger the smells became. He also felt somewhat foolish for being suspicious of the fact he could smell that something other than wood had been burned.

The structure was a barn, after all. Barns held a lot of animals. Even the empty ones tended to be filled by mice, birds, dogs or anything else looking for shelter.

When the large figure exploded from within the barn, Clint had just taken his hand away from his gun. He hadn't heard anything coming, and he sure as hell hadn't expected something so big to fly at him so fast. Before he had any notion of what was happening, Clint felt something slam into his midsection and knock all the wind from his lungs.

"You've been following me," the large man growled.

Now that Clint could get a better look at the figure, the term "large" just didn't quite seem to do him justice. The man's legs looked more like thick roots extending from an even thicker trunk of a torso. The man's face was clean-shaven and composed of deep lines that seemed to have been carved into his head. What caught Clint's attention more than anything, however, was the man's eyes. They were dark and just as lifeless as the scorched building from which he'd come.

"You're dead," the man grunted.

After glancing at the man for less than two seconds, Clint already knew well enough that he meant those two words he'd just uttered.

TWENTY-FIVE

Clint was knocked down with ease. By the time his backside hit the ground, his Colt had cleared leather. But no matter how fast his draw was, Clint felt his hand get slapped aside before he could take proper aim.

It wasn't as though Voorhees was faster than Clint. The bigger man was simply fearless and didn't waste one moment in considering what might happen if that gun went off in his face. The Colt did fire a shot, but it sent its round through the blackened wall to Clint's left.

"You're the lawman," Voorhees said in a deep, calm voice. "One of the lawmen that's been chasing me." As he spoke, he grabbed Clint's shoulder and lifted him an inch or so off the ground before slamming him back down again. "I don't run from nobody, you hear? I don't run from nobody."

Clint tried to speak in his own defense, but he could barely pull in enough air to make more than a strained wheezing sound.

Clint tried to take aim with the Colt, but soon regretted that decision when Voorhees balled up his fist, cocked his arm back and punched Clint's elbow. The blow was not only unexpected, but powerful enough to make Clint release his grip on the pistol.

While Clint's left arm wasn't quite as strong as his right,

it was the only one he could move quickly enough to do something before Voorhees hit him again. Fueled more by desperation than anything else, Clint took a wild swing that connected with Voorhees's leg.

The bigger man winced and grunted, but immediately prepared to hit Clint again. Seeing that reaction was all Clint needed to adjust his aim and swing his arm again.

This time, the side of Clint's fist hit Voorhees's knee like a hammer knocking into a post. Nothing snapped or gave way, but Voorhees lowered the fist he was about to throw so he could grab hold of his knee. As much as Clint wanted to do more, he used the precious second or two he'd just earned to roll out of the bigger man's reach.

Clint's eyes immediately spotted his pistol, which was lying a yard or two away. He then shifted his focus back to the big man in front of him. "This is some kind of mistake," Clint said. "I don't even know who you are."

"Then why are you here?" Voorhees asked in a voice that didn't show the slightest hint of exertion. "Why did you come after me?"

"There was a fire," Clint explained. "That's all. What are you doing here?"

Voorhees stared down at him as if he was staring straight through Clint and staring at something two miles behind him. Slowly, his head cocked to one side as his eyes made a downward trek. When he got to the holster at Clint's side, Voorhees asked, "Why bring a gun if you're just checking on a fire?"

"Because there's snakes out here. Not to mention big fellows who knock the stuffing out of me."

For a moment, it seemed that Clint's lighthearted tone might have actually rubbed off on Voorhees. Before the bigger man lowered his guard, however, his eyes narrowed and he stooped down toward Clint. "What's that in your pocket?"

Clint reached for his shirt pocket, but already knew what the big man might have seen. Sure enough, when he touched that spot on his shirt, he felt where the badge Henry had given him was snagged. It must have gotten jostled when he was knocked over, but Clint knew that might be enough to do him in.

"You are a lawman," Voorhees snarled. "I knew it."

All this time, Clint had moved slowly to get his feet under him without provoking the bigger man. Now that he could stand up again, he did so and took a few cautious steps back. "You could already be in a lot of trouble for attacking me that way," Clint said sternly. "But I'm willing to let it pass if you tell me why you're hiding out here."

"You're just looking for that other one," Voorhees said.

Clint did his best to keep his voice level when he asked, "Where is he? What did you do to him?"

But Voorhees wasn't about to be cowed by a stern voice. On the contrary, he grinned and stalked forward while balling his fists into tight knots of muscle and bone. A low growl started in the back of his throat and turned into a roar as Voorhees lashed out with a powerful swing.

If Clint had stayed where he was, his head might very well have been knocked clean off his shoulders. But Clint knew better than to stand in front of a steam engine, and he sure as hell wasn't going to stand in front of Voorhees. Ducking down low, Clint narrowly avoided that punch while also drawing the knife he kept in his boot.

The little knife wasn't much of a weapon, but it was better than nothing, and Clint put all his muscle behind it when he delivered a swing of his own. It had been a reflex to draw the blade with his right hand, but Clint quickly found that arm still aching from the earlier blow Voorhees had landed.

Clint's blade cut through the front of Voorhees's shirt and raked along the bigger man's midsection. It didn't cut too deeply before it hit a wall of muscle. Without even flinching at the cut, Voorhees twisted his upper body around and slammed his left forearm into Clint's side.

The impact of Voorhees's arm was similar to getting hit by an uprooted tree. Clint braced for it as best he could, but that wasn't enough to keep him from being knocked down. Hitting the ground only added to the dull aches that were piling up on his body. Fortunately, Clint was able to salvage something from the exchange.

Propping himself up on one arm, he reached out with the other to grab for the Colt that he'd lost earlier. As he strained to get ahold of the weapon, Clint could feel the impact of Voorhees's boots thumping against the dirt as the big man closed the distance between them.

"Gimme that badge," Voorhees snarled.

Clint threw himself forward and dropped his hand onto the Colt. As he rolled on his side, Clint was already bringing the gun up and tightening his finger around the trigger. His gun stopped short of its target as Voorhees rushed another step forward to drop his leg down like a brick wall.

Clint's wrist knocked against Voorhees's leg. The Colt went off. His bullet hissed away into thin air.

"I said gimme that badge."

Clint didn't say anything to that. He was still trying to figure out how Voorhees had moved so damn fast. Without wasting any more time, he rolled backward and prepared to take another shot. Even before he'd come out of his roll, Clint could hear Voorhees running after him.

The moment Clint was more or less upright, he fired toward him. That shot came close to the mark, but didn't draw any blood. Clint's next shot was taken a split second after the first, which was enough time for him to get himself situated and pick a better target. It wasn't, however, enough time to put Voorhees down.

The bigger man twitched when the bullet drilled through the meat of his upper thigh, but he didn't slow down. In fact, his movement wasn't impeded any more than if he'd gotten poked with a stick. Voorhees must have felt something from the gunshot, because he bared his teeth and let out a low grunt.

Clint was squeezing his trigger again when Voorhees stepped right up to him and swatted at his gun arm once more. The palm of Voorhees's hand felt like petrified wood and sent a jolt of pain all the way up to Clint's shoulder. The Colt bucked against Clint's palm, but it fired more or less straight into the air.

This time, Clint held onto the pistol with every bit of strength he could muster. Unfortunately for him, Clint felt Voorhees's fist clamp around his own hand as well as the gun, to encompass both of them with his meaty grasp.

"I won't let you shoot me again," Voorhees said in a surprisingly calm voice. "Now hand over that badge."

"Who are you?" Clint asked. "Tell me and I'll—"

"You'll what?" Voorhees asked as he savagely batted his hand across Clint's face.

All thoughts of fighting smart or getting information flew out the window the moment that slap landed. Clint didn't care if he had his gun or not. He was not about to just stand by and be swatted like a bug. Balling up his left fist, he swung with every ounce of strength he had. Clint's fist connected solidly, but still bounced off Voorhees's ribs like they were a slab of beef.

Before he could even feel that punch against his knuckles, Clint swung his right foot forward to slam against Voorhees's shin. He could see a wince on the bigger man's face, but kicked him in the same spot just to press the matter further.

Now that Voorhees was pulling Clint's arm almost hard enough to tear it from its socket, Clint had to put his foot down to maintain some of his balance. Almost immediately, Clint raised his other leg to bring his knee crashing into Voorhees's groin.

Being a man himself, Clint was reluctant to hit that spot unless it was absolutely necessary. Even so, he should have done it way before the scales got tipped so far out of his favor.

Also being a man, Voorhees grunted and winced when Clint's knee found its mark. He started to double over, but then forced his eyes open to look at Clint with a stare that would have been at home on the face of the devil himself.

Clint managed to pull his fist out of Voorhees's grasp. The moment he regained control of his Colt, however, Clint also felt something similar to being kicked in the stomach by an angry mule. The impact doubled Clint over and lifted both boots off the ground. He thought some blood might have jumped into the back of his throat, but he was more concerned with the fact that he couldn't breathe.

Glaring down at Clint, Voorhees watched him hack and wheeze. He then sent his fist down like a hammer to pound against the upper half of Clint's gun arm and send the Colt

once more to the ground. From there, he rained down one
hammer after another until Clint was sprawled in the dirt.

Although part of Clint had a vague notion of what was
happening, he couldn't do anything to stop it. He could
barely even fill his lungs enough to keep from suffocating.
When Voorhees flopped him onto his back and grabbed him
by the throat, Clint thought it was the end of his time on this
earth.

TWENTY-SIX

Clint didn't die, but he couldn't move either. At least, not right away.

With a great amount of effort, Clint pulled in half a breath and rolled onto his stomach. The pain that ignited in his ribs, arms and chest was more than enough to get his limbs beneath him and lift him partly off the ground. Once he was on all fours, Clint felt another splash of something against the back of his throat and opened his mouth to spit out the vomit that had collected there.

He wasn't too sick, but those motions reminded him of how badly his stomach had been pummeled by the bigger man. Every muscle had been tensed, only to receive a beating that felt as if it was still happening. Knowing that he wasn't going to feel any better crawling back to town, Clint gritted his teeth against the pain and hauled himself to his feet.

Halfway up, Clint remembered the face of the man who'd dropped him. That thought lit a fire in Clint's belly that not only got him walking back to where he'd left Eclipse, but forced him to walk tall the entire way. As he made his way to the spot he'd seen the Darley Arabian, Clint reached for the holster at his side.

It was empty.

That discovery stopped him in his tracks.

Clint kept his hand on the empty leather and turned around quickly enough to send another wave of pain through his entire body. The last time he'd seen his gun, it was getting knocked from his hand as if it was nothing more than a bothersome toy. He almost didn't know what to think when he saw the Colt lying right where it should have landed.

Keeping perfectly still, Clint shifted his eyes to look around for any sign of the bigger man. Surely, the monster wouldn't have just walked away and left Clint with his gun in sight. Clint became even more confused when he felt his gun belt and found the loops were still mostly filled with spare ammunition.

It had to be a trap.

Didn't it?

Clint walked toward the gun cautiously. Part of him was expecting to be ambushed along the way or have some sort of trap sprung once he got there. But he made it all the way to the Colt without incident. In fact, the area seemed completely dead.

It was a bad choice of phrase, but accurate all the same. Although it hurt his battered body, Clint bent down to snatch up the Colt as quickly as possible. Once it was in his hand, he held it at the ready and turned to get a look all the way around him.

There was nobody coming.

There was nobody in sight.

As far as he could tell, there wasn't a living thing in the range of his pistol.

For the moment, that suited Clint just fine. Then again, another possibility jumped to his mind that made Clint shudder. Drawing in a painful breath, he let it out in a whistle that was aimed at the barn.

The next few quiet moments put a feeling of dread into Clint's belly. That feeling passed as soon as he heard hooves thumping against the ground and saw Eclipse trot from his spot around the back of the barn.

"Good to see you, boy," Clint said as he scratched the Darley Arabian behind the ears. "I thought he might have gotten to you, too." Just to be certain, Clint did a quick check of the stallion's head, torso and legs.

"Looks like you're all right," Clint said. "At least something went right."

It wasn't an easy task, but Clint pulled himself up into the saddle. Once there, he checked the Colt once more and found it to be exactly the way he'd left it, spent rounds and all. After replacing the empty shells with fresh bullets, Clint holstered the pistol and took another look around.

Something seemed strange.

Despite being glad to be alive and relatively well, Clint couldn't help but wonder why the big man would leave him that way after clearly gaining the upper hand.

When he thought back to what little the man had said, Clint realized what he should be looking for. He reached up for his shirt pocket, even though he knew what he would find. Sure enough, the badge Henry had given him was gone.

Clint didn't bother looking around for the badge. He knew he wouldn't find it. What he needed to do was find the man who'd taken it, and he needed to be quick about it.

TWENTY-SEVEN

Clint made it back to Solace, despite the fact that every bump along the way felt like another punch to his stomach. By the time he hitched Eclipse to the post outside of the Archer Hotel, Clint was becoming accustomed to the constant pain every breath cost him. He must have looked nearly as bad as he felt, since he attracted plenty of troubled stares on his way into the hotel and up to Bower's room.

After knocking on the door, Clint pushed the door open as soon as the Texas Ranger took a peek outside.

"Jesus Christ, Clint," Bower said as he stepped aside and then shut the door after Clint had entered. "What the hell happened to you?"

"Where's Mark?" Clint asked.

"You look like you went through hell."

"Where's Mark?"

"He's in the room across the hall," Bower replied. "That way, we can hear if someone's coming, or the other can get behind someone if they—"

Not too interested in Bower's strategy, Clint left the room and stepped across the hall. He knocked on the door and heard steps on the other side of it. "Open up, Mark. It's Clint Adams."

The door came open. When Clint got a look at the face of

the man who'd opened it, he thought he might be looking into a mirror. Mark's face was bruised and bloodied. His eyes were somewhat vacant, but that could be explained by the stench of whiskey on his breath.

"What the hell happened to you?" Clint asked.

Mark started to grin, but winced instead. "I could ask you the same thing."

Just then, Bower placed his hand on Clint's shoulder and pushed him toward the door. Clint reacted quickly and almost knocked Bower into a wall in his haste to shake free of the younger man's hand.

"I've been shoved around too much today," Clint said.

Bower held up his hands and stepped forward again. "Fine, but let's take this inside. There's too many folks checked into this hotel, and I don't want to conduct business where any of them can hear."

Mark opened the door all the way so Clint and Bower could enter. The room looked similar to Bower's, except for the half-empty bottle of whiskey sitting next to a basin filled with bloody water. "Unless you fell off your horse and landed on a rock," Mark said, "my guess is you crossed paths with the same man I did."

"Tall guy who could have taken a hit from a train?" Clint asked.

Mark grinned and displayed a bloody set of teeth. "That's the one."

"Where'd you find him?"

"I went to get a look at the barn that burned down," Mark explained. "It didn't look like anyone was killed, so I thought the fire was just an accident. When I was looking around inside, that big fellow cornered me. At first, I didn't think he was going to be a problem. He didn't even have a gun."

Bower swore under his breath. "I shouldn't have let you go on your own. I should've been there."

"No offense," Clint said, "but I doubt you would've done much good if you were there. That is, unless you're in the habit of shooting first and asking questions later."

Bower shrugged and shook his head. "Either one of you would have stood a better chance if you weren't alone."

"And either one of us could have insisted that you come along," Clint added. "So it's all of our fault. Go on with what you were saying, Mark."

"There's not much else to say. He walked up to me and I started asking him a few questions. Just as I was getting suspicious, he grabbed hold of me and knocked me around so bad that I could barely move."

"Do you think he was the man we were after?" Bower asked. "There's plenty of crazy men living out on their own."

"He was the one," Mark replied. "He said he knew we'd been after him and that we weren't about to take him in."

"Did he ask for your badge?" Clint asked.

Mark lowered his head and nodded. "Yeah," he said shamefully. "And he got it, too."

"Don't feel so bad," Clint told him. "He got mine, too."

"You don't have a badge," Bower pointed out.

"Henry gave me one to help make things easier for me. Turns out it was worse than raw meat hanging around my neck."

Bower shook his head and grumbled, "Henry's not going to like this one bit. Not only did we find this killer and let him get away, we let him take two Texas Ranger badges in the process. Those badges can be put to some mighty bad purposes, you know."

Clint looked at the young lawman and silenced him with a glare. "I know," he said. "But that big fellow won't have those badges for long. I intend on taking them back as soon as I can."

"Sure. If we ever catch up to him. He's got to be miles away by now."

"He didn't go anywhere," Clint said under his breath.

"And what's going to stop him?" Mark asked. "I don't mean any offense either, but none of us did much good by standing in his way."

Nodding as much as his aching head would allow, Clint said, "Which is exactly why he won't go anywhere just yet."

"You think he's gonna start another fire?" Mark asked.

Clint kept nodding. "After what I've heard and seen of this killer, he won't be happy just lighting up an abandoned barn. I'd wager he's got something else planned that'll harm plenty more than just some field mice. He's also feeling pretty good about himself right about now."

"Hell," Mark grunted. "If I'd put a beating on someone like the one I got, I'd be feeling damn near untouchable."

"Which is why he's still gonna do his business here, and he's probably going to do it real soon."

Glancing between the other two, Bower asked, "Are either of you in any condition to help catch him or should I go fetch Henry?"

"I'd die rather than crawl into a hole and lick my wounds so that asshole can do what he pleases," Clint said.

Mark winced and spit out some blood before climbing back to his feet. "Where do we start?"

TWENTY-EIGHT

Clint's first priority was to get back on his feet and moving at a fairly steady pace. After a few attempts where he was forced to take a moment or two to catch his breath, he got familiar enough with his pain to make it work for him. Every wince was a spur in his side and every stumble was turned into a forward step.

Once he was on the street with the other Rangers beside him, Clint thought about the question Mark had asked before they'd left. While pondering where they should start looking for the big man, Clint did some thinking as to where the man could be headed. Before too long, that line of thought lifted Clint's eyes upward.

"It won't be dark for a while yet," Clint said.

Bower looked up as well, but didn't seem to know why he was doing it. "What's that matter?"

"Unless you know otherwise, I'd say this man doesn't set a fire unless it's dark or close to it," Clint replied.

"How can you say that for certain?"

Clint shrugged. "He likes fire, and fire looks a lot more impressive at night than during the day."

Looking at his partner with a wary smile on his face, Mark said, "I didn't think of that because I got my head kicked in. What's your excuse?"

"Keep up the smart-ass comments and you'll get it kicked in again."

"We have a bit of time to kill," Clint said. "I could use a drink. How about you?"

"I've never needed a drink more than I do right now," Mark grumbled.

Bower stepped between them and pointed toward a saloon at the nearest corner. "I'm buying."

Clint wasn't about to refuse an offer like that, so he and the two Texas Rangers stepped into the saloon and ordered their drinks. Although Mark went straight for the whiskey to take the edge off his pain, Clint ordered a beer and a cup of water.

A few sips of beer helped dull the agony that filled Clint's body, but it was the water that truly felt heaven-sent. The cold water trickled down his throat, making him wince and sigh in relief at the same time. It may not have chased away as much pain as whiskey might have, but it cleared up his vision and brought his wits right back to where they needed to be.

"Where do we go from here?" Bower asked. "Did either of you hear what the killer intended to do next?"

"I don't think we need too many guesses to figure it out," Mark replied.

Clint set down his water and stood up from his chair. "He's right. And since it'll be dark before too much longer, we should get out and start walking the streets."

"Where are we going?" Bower asked.

"I intend on covering as much ground as we can and making as much noise as possible along the way."

Bower and Mark both looked confused.

Seeing their expressions, Clint led the way out of the saloon so the other two would follow him. "The time for sneaking around is over," he told the two Rangers. "That killer knows he's being tracked, and he's not worried about it. What we need to do is take the wind from his sails and show him we won't be deterred so easily."

"How do you intend on doing that?" Mark asked.

"By walking the streets. By being seen and heard. That's how."

"And you think he'll be watching?"

"He didn't get this far not being caught without keeping an eye out for the likes of us. Once he sees us out and about as if none of his punches landed, he'll come out from wherever he's at to finish what he started."

All three of them were standing on the boardwalk outside of the saloon. Clint stretched his arms and started walking just as he'd said he would. Bower and Mark walked alongside him, but they didn't seem too eager to be there.

The Rangers followed Clint down the street. They shot anxious glances at each other and then shot some impatient glances at Clint. When they reached a corner and saw Clint come to a stop, Mark and Bower seemed ready to jump out of their skins.

That condition worsened once Clint found a spot next to a post at the corner, leaned back and crossed his arms.

"What's the meaning of this, Adams?" Bower snapped.

"That's the way," Clint replied. "Nice and loud. Just like that."

"To hell with that! You'll answer my question!"

"Weren't you listening before?" Clint asked. "We're going to draw him out before he gets a chance to do what he's intending on doing."

"And what's that?"

Clint scowled at Bower before saying, "If I need to tell you that, then you really haven't been paying attention."

"I know he starts fires. I know he kills. God damn it, Adams, we've been chasing this bastard a hell of a lot longer than you!"

Mark stepped in between them before Bower made one wrong move too many. "I think we all know what we're dealing with, Clint. It's just that this asshole tends to set his fires out away from a town, so even though seeing us may draw him out, he may not be anywhere near this spot."

"Oh, he's near this spot," Clint said.

"Oh, is he? Did he mention where he was going to be when he was pounding your face in? Because he didn't say a word about it when he was kicking in mine."

Clint turned to look at Mark, but he wasn't upset with the

young lawman. In fact, Mark was the only one around who could have gotten away with saying that to him at that moment.

"He's right around here," Clint stated confidently. "And he's probably close enough to have seen or heard us by now. You want to know how I know?"

"Yes," Bower replied. "Just spit it out."

"You sure you don't know already?"

Mark pulled in a deep breath to calm his nerves. Suddenly, his eyes snapped open and he reached out to slap a hand on Bower's shoulder. All the while, Mark kept pulling in one quick breath after another.

"What's wrong with you?" Bower asked.

"Take a breath."

"I don't need to take a breath. I'm just fine with—"

Cutting Bower off by gripping his shoulder even tighter, Mark repeated himself through gritted teeth. "Take a breath."

Bower took a breath. It didn't take long before his expression changed and he looked across the street.

Mark was also looking across the street as his hand drifted to the gun hanging at his side. Neither of the Texas Rangers was speaking. They were too busy pulling air in through their noses.

"I believe we're all on the same page now, gentlemen," Clint proclaimed.

"That smell," Mark whispered. "Is it . . . ?"

"Yep," Clint said. "It sure is. Kerosene."

TWENTY-NINE

Now that they were standing still and facing the right direction, they could all smell the odor of kerosene drifting through the air. Once the wind shifted direction, Clint could hardly take a full breath without feeling his head start to swim.

"When did you find this?" Bower asked.

"On our way to that saloon," Clint replied.

"And how is it that none of these people can smell it?"

Clint looked up and down the street at the people Bower was referring to. Although some of them cast a glance or two at the buildings, most of them wound up shifting their eyes to one of the few lamps on the side of the street. "They do," he said. "They just don't know what to make of it."

"Forget about them," Mark said. "How is it that we missed this before? I must have walked straight past this building at least twice earlier today."

"That kerosene wasn't out here before," Clint said more as a way of thinking out loud. "It couldn't have been."

Bower nodded and cocked his head slightly to one side. "You're right. Someone would have noticed it or even sparked it long ago if there'd been that much kerosene around. As a matter of fact, I think I see where it's at."

"Good," Clint replied with a sudden sense of urgency. "Because if we know how far along it's spread, we can start to warn folks. I've been trying to get a look at what buildings have been doused."

"Those," Bower replied as he raised a finger to point across the street.

Mark looked that way and squinted. "Which ones?"

"Near as I can tell . . . all of them."

"All right. You two head over there and split up," Clint told them. "Show your badges, shout as loud as you can, just try to get as many folks as possible away from those buildings."

"But we're not the law here," Mark reminded him.

"Once you shout what's about to happen and wave around any piece of tin, folks will follow your orders. Just try to direct them away from there before things get too crazy."

Mark and Bower settled a few quick things between themselves before charging forward and shouting that the buildings were about to go up in flames. That was more than enough to get folks moving. In fact, it was more than enough to create a stampede.

As much as Clint would have liked to keep things a little better organized, there was no way to make that happen on such short notice. The best he could do was hang back a ways and make sure nobody got trampled. Fortunately, the two Texas Rangers were doing a fairly good job of keeping the locals moving in an orderly fashion. That left Clint to keep his eyes peeled for another face amid the crowd.

Amazingly enough, Clint didn't spot Voorhees right away. What caught his eye was a little flicker of flame coming from somewhere a bit too close to one of the doused buildings. The moment Clint saw that spark, he ran straight toward it.

Voorhees stood in the shadow of one of the buildings with a bunch of matches in his hand. He'd already struck the matches and now was about to toss them onto the wall of a general store.

"Toss those matches away," Clint shouted, "or I'll gun you down where you stand!"

While Clint had thought the big man would want to kill him on sight, he couldn't have been more wrong.

Unlike most men who made a try for Clint Adams, Voorhees hadn't tried to kill the Gunsmith in order to put a feather in his cap. He'd just been taking out another obstacle in his path. His true passion was the fire in his hands, which was about to ignite an entire building before spreading to engulf the whole street.

Voorhees barely seemed interested that Clint was alive or dead. He hardly seemed to acknowledge Clint was there. Instead, he held onto the matches in one hand while reaching out to snag a woman by the arm with the other.

And then, after pulling the woman in front of him like she was a rag doll, Voorhees showed Clint a lifeless, predator's smile and looked down at the kerosene-soaked spot at his feet.

"Oh my God," Clint whispered as he realized the big man was going to light that fire whether it meant getting shot or even standing in the middle of the inferno.

With the same effort he might toss away an old newspaper, Voorhees threw down the bundle of lit matches.

THIRTY

Clint drew his Colt and pulled the trigger in a flicker of motion. The gun in his fist blazed several times in quick succession, spitting out a flurry of hot lead in a tight cluster.

It seemed to take forever for the bullets to cross the street, but in that time Clint found himself thanking God that the other man was so damn tall.

The matches fell from Voorhees's hand and headed straight for the puddle of kerosene he'd poured. He was watching the matches so closely that he saw the exact moment when Clint's bullets found the matches and snuffed out all of them except for one.

"*No!*" Voorhees snarled as he shoved the woman aside and stomped toward Clint.

Clint ran across the street as well. He kept his back straight until the last possible moment, when he ducked down low to avoid Voorhees's arm that swung at him like a scythe toward a field of wheat. Clint kept right on running until he made it across the street to where that single match had landed. The little flame had stayed alive just long enough to make its landing and ignite a trickle that had run away from the main pool of kerosene.

"I'll kill you!" Voorhees bellowed as he wheeled around and stomped back at Clint. Every step the big man took was faster than the one before it, and he reached Clint before Clint could lower the boot he'd raised up over the kerosene.

Although he was facing away from Voorhees, Clint was all too familiar with the bigger man's speed. He turned his Colt to one side and then swung his arm to catch Voorhees in the stomach with the Colt's handle. The blow didn't send Voorhees back, but it stopped him in his tracks just long enough for Clint to stomp out the flame before it could truly get going.

"All right," Clint said once the flame was dead. "Now it's your turn."

The big man gritted his teeth and swung at Clint with a fist that seemed more like a knotted clump of wood. Clint ducked beneath the swing and leaned away from the one behind it. The bigger man's fists cut through the air and made just enough noise to let Clint know how much raw power was behind each one.

Knowing that he couldn't win a fistfight with Voorhees, Clint brought his Colt around to fire the last shot in its cylinder. Somehow, Voorhees caught Clint's wrist before the gun could be pointed at him. Clint kept from wasting his bullet and put every bit of his muscle behind the effort of moving the gun to give him any shot whatsoever.

Voorhees kept one hand on Clint's wrist and then clamped the other around the back of his neck. From there, the big man leaned forward and let out a slow, controlled breath.

"You should've stayed away," Voorhees growled. "You would have lived to see this. Now you'll just have to die here like all these others."

No matter how much he tried to move his gun arm in the opposite direction, Clint felt it being pushed toward the kerosene-soaked side of the street. Even worse was the fact that he was being forced to aim at the woman Voorhees had been holding captive when Clint had first spotted him.

Clint locked eyes with the woman and shouted in a voice that sounded more like a howl. "Move away from there!"

The woman looked at Clint with eyes full of fear. She seemed rooted to her spot at first, but ran quickly enough when she saw the Colt slowly moving to point at her.

Clint kept fighting against Voorhees, but the other man was too strong. Not only was the bigger man forcing Clint to shift his aim, but he was dragging Clint even closer to the other side of the street. Within a few seconds, Clint felt Voorhees's finger settle over the one resting on the Colt's trigger.

"Fire!" someone shouted nearby. "There's gonna be a fire!"

Clint let out part of the breath he'd been holding when he heard that voice. Just as he'd hoped, the warning was followed by the stampede of footsteps as folks ran to get as far away from that side of the street as possible. Silently praising Mark and Bower for their quick work, Clint focused all of his efforts into his more immediate problem.

Voorhees looked up at the herd of people running from the building as well. The expression he wore was like night and day when compared to Clint's. Instead of relief, Voorhees showed anger. Before too long, that anger turned into rage.

A gunshot cracked through the air to whip past Voorhees's shoulder and Clint's head. Voorhees paid as much attention to that as he would to a wasp buzzing near his cheek.

Letting out a final grunt, Voorhees put every last bit of his strength into pushing Clint's gun arm toward the closest building. He was simply too strong for Clint to resist. The next thing Clint felt was Voorhees's finger crushing his own finger as well as the trigger beneath it.

The modified Colt bucked against Clint's palm and sent its last round into the nearby boardwalk. Since Voorhees had shoved Clint to within a yard of the boardwalk, the sparks from the gun also ignited the kerosene pooled there.

Voorhees placed his palm over Clint's face the way a child grabbed a ball, and shoved Clint toward the fire. The moment Clint was clear of the bigger man, more shots were fired from the two men to Clint's left. But Clint didn't see where Voorhees went or who was doing the shooting. He was too concerned with pulling off his jacket and using it to smother the flames.

The gunshots were still coming, and they were even getting louder as Clint kept batting down the flames.

What started as a crackle turned into a roar as the flames

got to the kerosene before Clint could get to them. Even as the heat grew worse and worse around him, Clint wouldn't stop trying to put out the fire. Even as the gunshots sounded from directly behind him, Clint kept swinging his jacket at the fire.

"I think I hit him!" Mark shouted from behind Clint.

Bower fired another shot before saying, "He ducked into that alley. You stay behind and help Clint."

"No!" came another voice. "I can help."

Clint turned to find the woman who'd been Voorhees's prisoner a few moments ago rushing up to him. She waved at the people gathered nearby and shouted, "Come on! We can all help before this fire spreads!"

That got the others moving. Some went for water and some rushed over to Clint's side. The Texas Rangers nodded and started to run toward the alley they'd been firing at.

"We'll be back, Clint," Bower said. He then shifted his eyes toward Mark and shouted, "You head straight that way and I'll circle around." After that, the men were out of Clint's sight.

The fire wasn't out of control, but it wasn't in control either. Every time Clint swatted out a portion of it, another blaze would be sparked to life. Already, the sparks had spread out beyond Clint's reach. He knew that it wouldn't be long before some of it would get away from him and set an inferno in motion.

"I've got this one," the woman said as she stomped her feet against the edge of a kerosene puddle before it could fully ignite.

Clint looked at her and didn't know if he should push her away or let her keep stomping her feet. Then, he saw one flicker of light a few inches out of his reach. The little flame raced toward the spot where the kerosene became thicker and spread out. An instant later, all he could hear was the roar of a real fire gaining its strength.

"Over there! Over there!" someone shouted.

Clint turned to see a row of four men carrying buckets rush up to the blaze and douse it with water. Some sand was dropped down, followed by more water, which was enough to bury the fire and kerosene in wet mud.

Only then did Clint allow himself to step back and take in the rest of his surroundings.

To his surprise, there were a lot more than just a few locals gathered in the street. By the looks of it, nearly all the ones who'd run out of the stores and businesses had stuck around to help put out the fire. A small line of folks had already formed to carry water from some of the troughs near the hitching posts, in buckets that were emptied onto the boardwalk.

One of the men sported a large mustache that was thick enough to droop down and cover his mouth. "Step aside, ma'am," he said as he gently eased the woman back. "We'll have this out in no time."

Clint and the woman stepped away as more water was dumped onto the boardwalk. "You'd better wash down all those buildings," he said to one of the men in the bucket line. "There's kerosene on all of them."

"I thought I smelled something," the man with the mustache replied.

THIRTY-ONE

Clint was more than happy to let the locals put out the fire so he could see about catching Voorhees. "Which way did those other two men go?" Clint asked the woman who'd stepped in to help him earlier.

"That alley," she replied. "Right over there."

After giving his quick thanks to her, Clint rushed to the alley. Considering how fast everyone had been moving, he wasn't too surprised to find the alley completely empty. Clint ran down it anyway and had his gun reloaded by the time he came out the other side.

The alley emptied into another street, which was also empty. Just looking from his left to his right, Clint could see at least half a dozen places Voorhees or the Texas Rangers could have gone. Rather than pick a direction and hope for the best, Clint walked back to the spot where the bucket brigade had been formed.

The flames were out, and a row of men was making its way down the street to clean off the rest of the buildings. Clint spotted the woman he'd talked to a little earlier at one of the troughs, filling buckets to hand over to the brigade.

She was a tall, full-figured woman with dark red hair. Although her face was smudged by smoke at the moment, it was clear to see she had a smooth, creamy complexion underneath the grime. When she saw Clint, she smiled and waved before excusing herself from the trough. As soon as she stepped aside, her spot was filled by another local who was eager to help.

"Are you all right?" she asked as she rushed over to Clint.

"I came back to ask you that question."

"Well, I wasn't the one who sent that madman running."

"No," Clint replied. "You were the one who was grabbed up by that madman. I hope he didn't hurt you."

She shook her head. "No," she replied breathlessly. It didn't take long for her to add, "But he did scare the daylights out of me."

"Did he say anything to you?"

"He told me he wanted to see me burn. That's all."

"You're certain?" Clint asked.

The woman closed her eyes and looked down as she nodded. "I'm certain. I'll remember those words for the rest of my life. I thought they were going to be the last ones I'd ever hear."

"Well . . . they weren't." After hearing those words come from his mouth, Clint had to hang his own head and laugh. "I probably could have thought of something more comforting than that, but I'm awfully tired."

She was laughing as well. "It's all right. I'd say you have a pretty good excuse."

"How about we get away from here? It seems like these folks have everything well in hand."

"I'd like that," she said.

"Excuse me," a man hollered from the bucket brigade. "Pardon me. Sir?"

Clint looked for who was shouting and found a portly man with a long beard waving for his attention.

"Yes, you," the portly man said. "Could I have a word with you? It's about the man who set this fire."

"That's the town marshal," the woman told Clint. "And I don't think he's going to take no for an answer."

"I'd still like to—" Clint said before he was cut off once more by the portly fellow.

"I need a word with you, sir. Please. It's very important."

Stepping back before she was knocked aside by the town marshal, the woman told Clint, "My name is Janie McGowan. I'll wait for you at that restaurant right on the corner."

Clint turned to get a look at where she was pointing and saw the place. He nodded and turned back to find the marshal practically standing toe to toe with him.

"Fred Butters," the portly man announced as he took hold of Clint's hand and shook it. "Didn't mean to be rude, but I wanted to be sure and have a word with you before you got lost in all this commotion."

Looking over his shoulder, Clint saw Janie wave and walk toward the corner restaurant.

"That was a hell of a job you did, sir," Butters declared. "This whole town's in debt to you."

"My pleasure," Clint replied.

"Now I'd just like you to let us know what the hell happened." In a more intent tone, the marshal added, "I'd also like to know how you just happened to be in the right place at the right time. I don't believe I've seen you around here before."

"Look, I just . . ." Clint trailed off when he caught sight of someone in the corner of his eye. Bower and Mark spotted him at the same time and walked over to stand beside him.

"He's gone," Mark said. "God damn him, he moved too damn fast! I should have shot him when I had the chance."

"You tried, Mark," Bower said. "We both did. We just missed, is all. At least Clint had some better luck than we did. Hell of a good job, Adams."

Butters cleared his throat and raised his voice a notch. "That one's Adams, so who are you two? In fact, why don't you all just come with me and we can talk in my office?"

"How about we catch our breath first?" Mark snapped. "Is that all right with you?"

"Watch your mouth, boy. I'm the town marshal here, and for all I know, you men are the ones who had something to do with starting this fire."

Before Clint or Mark could get too bent out of shape, Bower stepped in to do the one thing neither of them could.

"It's all right," Bower said as he held out his badge. "These two are with me. I'll be glad to answer your questions."

"You're lawmen, huh?" Butters asked as he glanced at the badge. "Well, I suppose that's more like it."

THIRTY-TWO

Clint walked into the restaurant, found Janie's table and sat down. Letting out a tired breath, he said, "That marshal of yours is a real piece of work."

Janie laughed and poured Clint a cup of water from the pitcher that had been sitting on the table. "Hopefully he didn't give you too much trouble."

"He didn't, but it wasn't from lack of trying." Clint took the water and drank some. Although the cool liquid washed out the smoky taste from his mouth, Clint was getting awfully tired of breathing in soot.

"Do you know who that man was?" Janie asked.

"Yeah. And now that you mention him, I'd prefer it if we got away from this place. That man's got a nasty habit of tracking me down."

"We're safe here, aren't we? I mean, the law's right outside. Aren't you a lawman?"

"None of that means we're any safer in here. Considering I can still smell kerosene, I'd say it's unwise to push our luck any further."

Janie was reluctant to nod, but she did. She also forced a smile onto her face as she stood up. "I was hoping that man was long gone by now. Do you think he's still waiting out there?"

"I honestly don't know. Why don't I just see you home and make sure you get through your own door safe and sound?"

"All right. I'd appreciate that."

Clint offered her his arm and escorted her outside. There was still quite a large crowd in the street where the fire had been. He could also see Bower showing the town's marshal where he and Mark had chased Voorhees. Seeing the way Butters postured and strutted made Clint glad he wasn't forced to deal with the man himself.

"So where do you live?" Clint asked.

Janie started to answer, but found herself distracted by the blackened section of boardwalk where Voorhees had thrown his matches. "Oh," she said while snapping herself out of her thoughts. "My house is right down that street. I can make it there on my own, thanks."

"I'd much rather see to it you get there, since that man is still out there."

Keeping her head down, Janie nodded. "All right, then."

After walking a few more steps, Clint asked, "How did that man get ahold of you?"

"I was walking down the street and he just . . . grabbed me."

"And he said he wanted you to burn?"

"Yes. Why are you asking me this?"

Clint shrugged and kept walking. "Maybe I took in too much smoke. Must've fogged up my brain a little."

Janie smiled at that and stopped so she could stand directly in front of him. "I should be asking if you're all right. After all, you're the one who risked so much just to come and pull me out of there."

"Like I said before, I was already after that fellow. It's too bad you got in the way." Glancing up the street, Clint asked, "Is your house nearby?"

"Yes. You've done more than enough. Please, just go and get some rest. Do you have a place to stay?"

"Not yet."

"Well, you should try the Archer. They serve a wonderful breakfast."

Clint nodded. "I think I'll do that. Are you sure you don't mind walking the rest of the way on your own?"

"I'm sure. Thank you so much."

Just as Clint was starting to turn around so he could walk back to the Archer Hotel, he felt Janie tap him on the shoulder. When he turned around, he soon felt Janie's lips pressed against his own. The kiss took Clint by surprise, but not in an unpleasant way. He simply leaned into it and savored the touch of her lips for as long as it lasted.

"I'll check in on you tomorrow," she whispered. "If that's all right?"

"What man in his right mind would refuse an offer like that?" Clint asked.

She smiled and lowered her head as if she'd suddenly become shy. "I don't know, but I'm glad you didn't. Maybe we can have breakfast."

"Sounds wonderful. I'm pretty tired, so if I'm not there at a reasonable hour, just have someone rattle my cage a bit."

"All right, Clint. Thanks again for everything."

"You're more than welcome," Clint replied. He turned and walked away, smiling to himself as his thoughts raced like wildfire inside his head.

THIRTY-THREE

Voorhees stared out at the night sky and cursed under his breath. When he looked around at the buildings that were either dark or only lit by a lantern or two in a few windows, he swore again.

"What's the matter, darling?" Elizabeth asked as she came up behind him.

"It should be burning," Voorhees replied. "It should all be burning."

"I know. It wasn't your fault."

"That doesn't matter. It should . . ." The more he tried to talk, the more of an effort it became. The big man's jaw locked up and he clenched his fists in frustration.

Elizabeth reached out to stroke his cheek lovingly. "I know," she said soothingly. "I'm angry, too. All that planning to find the perfect spot and to put down all that kerosene, only to have it all go to waste."

"We can do it again. We wouldn't even need to get too much more kerosene. There ain't no way they could have washed it all away."

Easing her hand away from his cheek, Elizabeth began gently brushing it through his hair instead. "Not here. Not anymore."

Voorhees slapped her hand away and wheeled around so

he could glare straight into her eyes. "What do you mean? Why not here? Half this town is set to go up in a ball of fire!"

She looked around at the small room behind them. At the moment, they were both on the tiny balcony extending from the bedroom window. There was a rocker out there, which looked like a child's toy compared to the man standing beside it. Inside the room, there lay the bodies of the family who'd built the house that Voorhees had found.

"Keep your voice down," she said.

"There ain't nobody else alive in this damn house."

"I don't know that for sure. I only got the ones I could see."

Voorhees turned to look at the bodies in the bedroom. There were four of them in all: a man, his wife and two boys. Neither of the two children was old enough to have shaved his first whisker yet.

Curling his lip in an ugly sneer, Voorhees lowered his voice to a more acceptable level. "I don't like leaving a job like that half-finished."

"Neither do I. Now, did any of those lawmen see you come back here?"

Voorhees shook his head. "I lost them easy."

"Are you sure about that?"

"If they knew where I was, they'd be comin' after me. I saw that much in their eyes."

Elizabeth studied the big man's face for a few seconds before she nodded. "Good." When she felt Voorhees reach out to touch her, she pulled away and asked, "What do you think you're doing?"

He looked at her as if he was trying to figure out how a complicated machine worked. Then, he tried reaching out for her again.

"No," she snapped. "Not until we both get what we want."

"I want you. Right now."

Although she turned away as if coyly trying to keep him back, there was no mistaking the fierceness in her eyes when she wrapped her fingers around a small knife and brought it up to the man's throat.

"You keep pushing yourself on me and I'll gut you," she vowed. "Just like I gutted those pigs over there."

Voorhees glanced over to the family lying on the bed and propped against the wall. The sight of those innocent people didn't do much for him. The fire in Elizabeth's eyes, however, did plenty.

"You can try to gut me if you want," Voorhees said. "But if none of those lawmen could touch me, then I don't think you've got much of a chance."

Elizabeth caught sight of the spots of dried blood on the man's arms, shoulder and side. Some of that blood obviously came from wounds he'd gotten during the last couple of scrapes with the law. The rest of it could have come from any number of other sources. Her eyes stayed on that blood until she found herself gently brushing her blade along Voorhees's arm.

"We both want the same thing," she said.

"No, we don't. I want the fire. You want the killing."

Elizabeth shrugged. "Six of one, half a dozen of the other. It all boils down to the same thing."

"I want to see that street burn. It'll be the best fire I've ever made."

"Why settle for a street when you can burn an entire town?" she offered.

Voorhees raised his eyebrows and asked, "You think we could burn a whole town?"

"Yes, I do. There's a place not too far from here that's smaller and should light up real nicely. All we need to do is set things up the way we did here and that whole town should be on fire in a few minutes."

"I could go back to that street and do the same thing right now. Like I said, that kerosene has still gotta be there."

"Yes, but we can settle our other problems in the other town."

"What do you mean?" Voorhees asked.

"The man leading those Texas Rangers is staying in Solace. Once we leave this town, they'll probably head back there to figure out what to do next."

"And just to be certain, we can show up there."

Elizabeth nodded. "Now you're thinking. Once those lawmen are all in the same place, we can burn them up."

Grinning, Voorhees said, "I like it when lawmen scream."

"They'll scream and then they'll die. After that, anyone will think twice about coming after us. Even if they do, we'll have a big enough head start that they won't catch up to us for a good long while."

"That'll be a fire to see," Voorhees said wistfully.

"Yes, it will. And we'll both get what we want."

THIRTY-FOUR

Those killers were still nearby. Clint knew it. He could smell it. Actually, he could still smell kerosene, despite the fact that local business owners had been washing off their store-fronts all night long.

Clint, Mark and Bower were all in agreement that any arsonist wouldn't be so quick to leave when a fire was still within his grasp. Like any man with an obsession or strong desire, the killer would be chomping at the bit to finish what he'd started. It wasn't as if his plan had been completely spoiled.

All it would take was a spark thrown in the right direction.

One stray match from someone walking down the street could catch onto a smudge of kerosene remaining on the boardwalk to turn the street into an inferno. For that reason, Clint and the Texas Rangers had picked a good spot over-looking the street and would take turns keeping watch.

The danger would pass once all the kerosene had been washed away or the boards that were too soaked had been pulled up. There would also be reason to breathe easier if one of the marshal's men caught sight of the big killer trying to leave town. Butters seemed to be a better blowhard than he was a lawman, but Clint thought he was capable enough to watch the borders of his own town.

Bower insisted on taking the first shift of watching the street that was being cleaned up, and Mark offered to go next. That left Clint with a bit of time to himself in which he could rest up for whatever insanity might be coming.

There was a small bar in the restaurant of the Archer Hotel. Because of that, the place didn't feel like a restaurant, but it didn't quite feel like a saloon either. It seemed most folks preferred one or the other, which meant the hotel was fairly quiet. While that was bad for business, it was good for Clint's headache.

He sat at a small table with his back to the wall, nursing a beer and wondering if the kitchen would still be open this late at night. He was getting tired, but not tired enough for his eyes to play tricks on him. Even so, when he saw Janie McGowan walk through the lobby, he suspected he might have mistaken her for some other redhead.

Clint took his beer with him as he went to the doorway connecting the restaurant to the lobby. There may have been other redheads in town, but Janie's curves were unmistakable. Part of him even kicked around the notion of letting her keep walking just so he could watch her from behind.

"Is that you, Janie?" Clint asked from his spot in the doorway.

The redhead stopped with one foot perched upon the bottom of the staircase leading up to the guest rooms. She glanced over her shoulder and quickly spotted Clint. Smiling as she walked toward him, she immediately made Clint glad he'd rejected his first idea of letting her pass by.

Janie wore a different dress than the one she'd had on the last time he'd seen her. This dress wasn't tainted black by smoke or rumpled from her tussle with a would-be kidnapper, and it was obviously intended for use in the evening. It was made from dark purple velvet and cut down low enough in the front to show Clint plenty of the smooth, creamy skin of her breasts.

Her bottom lip was plump, and it curved into a warm smile as she got closer to him. When she spoke, it was in a voice that was just as smooth as her skin. "It sure is me," she said. "I was just coming by to see you."

"Well, you found me."

"And in good health, I see."

Clint nodded and motioned toward the restaurant behind him. "Today was a little rough, but nothing a bit of rest couldn't cure. Would you like to join me for a drink?"

"Sure. Are the rest of those men staying here as well? The ones from Texas, I believe?"

"They're right upstairs."

Janie glanced toward the stairs and then looked down. When she looked up again, there was no mistaking the promise in her eyes. "Actually, I was hoping to get you alone. It's been such a wild day. Maybe we could go for a walk?"

Clint nodded. "I could use some fresh air. Just let me settle up my bill and I'll be right with you."

It didn't take long for Clint to pay for his beers, but Janie wasn't in the lobby when he returned. All he had to do was step outside the hotel and he found her leaning against one of the posts lining the street. Hearing the hotel's door open got her to look over her shoulder. The moment she saw Clint, she smiled and took his arm.

"I have a confession to make," she said.

"That's not my line of work, but I'll do my best," Clint replied with a wink.

"I've been wanting to clear my head with a nice, long walk all night, but haven't felt safe enough to go anywhere."

"There's been plenty of lawmen in the streets after what happened," Clint said.

Janie shrugged. "None of them stepped up like you did. To be honest, I think you're the only one who stands a chance against that killer."

"Oh, I don't know about that."

"I know," she said. "I was there. I saw how you stood up to him. It made my blood warm up inside of me."

She kept walking arm in arm with Clint and led him around the next corner. They walked into a section of town that was away from the sounds and activity of the saloon district. In fact, it was so quiet along their path that they were the only ones out and about on that street.

Suddenly, Janie stopped and turned to face Clint. She was

tall enough to lean forward and kiss him without needing to pull herself up or make him come down to get to her. Before she could kiss him again, she saw one of the marshal's deputies come around the corner and walk toward them.

"And here I thought I'd get you to myself," she whispered.

"The marshal's men will be making their rounds all night to watch for the killer," Clint said.

"Then maybe we could go somewhere out of sight?"

"That sounds like a great idea to me."

"Good," Janie said with a smile. "I know just the place."

THIRTY-FIVE

The place where Janie took him was a small corral in the back of a fenced-in lot on a darkened corner. Since there were no lamps on the street and no lights in any of the nearby windows, Clint felt as if he'd left the town's limits altogether. There was hardly anything inside the small building where Janie took him, apart from a few bales of hay and an old mule in the far corner.

"Not quite alone," Clint said as he nodded toward the mule, "but it seems close enough."

"It's just fine," Janie said as she pressed herself against him and pulled Clint's shirt out from under the waistband of his pants. "Because I don't want to wait another second."

Janie's hands slipped under Clint's shirt and her fingernails raked against his skin. She kissed him urgently and even chewed gently on his bottom lip.

While Janie ran her tongue along Clint's mouth and unbuttoned his shirt, Clint was keeping busy as well. He moved his hands along her hips, sliding them all the way up until he could feel the ample curves of her breasts. He then eased his hands back down again to cup her plump backside.

Unbuckling Clint's belt, Janie let out a loud sigh. "It feels like you don't mind me being so forward," she said while stroking his erection through his jeans.

"Not in the least," Clint replied. "I hope you don't mind some of the same." Before he got a reply to that, Clint hiked up her skirts and slipped his hands beneath them.

Not only did Janie allow him to go on, but she leaned back and raised one leg to grant him easier access to the warm place between her legs.

Clint backed her up against a wall so Janie could wrap both her legs around him. Holding her up to waist level using both hands, Clint felt her mouth on his lips again and again as Janie became more and more excited. Finally, she brought her legs back down so she could stand on her own.

"Take that gun off," she ordered.

Clint smirked and unbuckled his belt. "Yes, ma'am."

Janie pulled his jeans down and grabbed onto his cock with both hands. She then dropped to her knees and sucked on him as if he was a stick of candy. As her head bobbed between his legs, she reached up to run her fingertips along his chest.

For a minute or two, Clint watched her lick and suck on him with a passion that only grew as time went by. He then reached down to grab her by the arms and help her to her feet.

Wearing a sexy pout, Janie said, "But I wasn't finished yet."

"Neither am I," he told her while turning her around. "Not by a long shot."

She looked over her shoulder and kept her eyes on him as she was turned around toward a stack of hay bales. When she felt Clint rub her hips through her dress, Janie arched her back and let out a slow moan. As soon as she felt Clint start to pull her skirts up again, Janie helped out by hiking them up around her waist and spreading her legs in a wide stance.

"Oh God, Clint. This is so . . ." Her breath along with the rest of her words was taken away when she felt Clint enter her from behind.

His rigid cock slid easily into her wet pussy. Clint held onto her hips with one hand, while holding her skirts up with other. She wore black stockings with little red bows at the back; both of which stood in stark contrast to her soft, luminescent skin. As he pushed all the way inside of her, he saw

Janie lean forward until she was almost resting her chest flat upon the bales of hay.

As Clint started pumping in and out of her faster, he looked down at the smooth, pale skin of her thighs. Her plump backside felt soft and warm as he bumped against her. When he slipped every last inch of his cock inside of her, he could feel Janie's body clenching around him.

"Yes," she whispered as she grabbed onto the hay bale. "Just like that. Don't stop."

Clint ran one hand along the small of Janie's back and kept his other hand on her backside. That way, when he pumped in and out of her, he could feel her squirming and wriggling against him. Before too long, she'd adjusted to his rhythm and began rocking back against him.

Propping herself up on her elbows, Janie tossed her red hair over one shoulder and looked back at Clint. She locked eyes with him and bared her teeth in something that was part smile and part snarl. When Clint buried his cock deep within her, she gritted her teeth and dug her fingers into the hay.

Clint pulled out of her and spun her around. Noticing how much she liked being handled that way, he didn't say a word before lifting her up so she could sit on the edge of the bales.

Spreading her legs open wide, Janie wrapped them around Clint's waist and pulled him in. She didn't kiss him, but stared up into his eyes as she guided his penis into her with both hands. Once he was inside, she leaned back and held herself up with both arms.

Lifting her skirts, Clint got a good look at the soft hair between Janie's legs. It was every bit as fiery as the hair on her head, making the skin of her inner thighs seem even more like fresh cream. As he eased into her, Clint saw Janie reach down to hold herself open for him.

Her fingers brushed against the lips of her pussy to allow him to penetrate her more easily. Rather than take her fingers away, she rubbed tiny circles around the little nub of her clitoris and moaned softly.

Clint drove into her a few times before sliding his hand along her leg. When he got close to her right knee, he saw Janie snap her eyes open and lean forward.

"Not there," she insisted in a breathy voice. Taking his hand in hers, she guided him back up to the bare skin between her legs. "There."

Allowing himself to be guided by her, Clint watched her expression change as his fingers brushed against her pussy. It would have been more accurate to say the expression she'd been wearing before melted into one of complete ecstasy.

Once Clint's hand was rubbing her the right way, Janie peeled down the front of her dress to reveal her breasts. They were small, but nicely curved. The skin of her nipples was so pale that it barely stood out. Her nipples were standing out plenty, however, and were hard to the touch.

Clint began sliding in and out of her in long, slow strokes. He pulled back until he was almost out of her before sliding all the way in again. When he buried himself in her, he moved his hand up along her belly to feel every one of her quick, excited breaths. From there, he moved his hand down again to feel her thigh.

Janie lay back and enjoyed what he was doing until she felt Clint's hand drift toward her knee. She immediately wrapped her legs around him and pumped her hips in a way meant to drive any man out of his mind.

While Clint couldn't ignore the effect she was having on him, he was intent on peeling down her stocking. Janie stopped him with a quick hand and a stern tone in her voice.

"I hurt my knee, Clint," she said while guiding his hand back between her thighs. "You touch me so good right there."

But Clint grinned and pulled his hand out of her grasp. He pumped into her once more, driving deep enough to take her breath away. Before she could fill her lungs again, he pulled down her right stocking to reveal the slender knife sheathed close to her knee.

"What about there?" he asked.

THIRTY-SIX

Janie made a grab for the knife that was almost quick enough. Despite his current situation between her legs, Clint was able to think straight enough to rip the knife away and tear the top of her stocking in the process.

But Janie wasn't through. She pulled in both legs and planted one foot against Clint's chest. After shoving him back, she attempted to drive her heel into Clint's chin. All Clint had to do was lean forward and a bit to one side in order to avoid the incoming kick. Once he was in between her legs again and pinning her against the hay bale, there wasn't a whole lot for her to do.

"Is this how you need to get a woman?" she snapped. "Force yourself on her in a dirty stable?"

Clint laughed and shook his head. "It wasn't my idea to come in here, and you seemed pretty happy about it a little while ago."

"Yeah, well a lot can change in a short amount of time."

"Yes," Clint said as he looked at the knife he'd found. "It sure can."

Scowling at him, Janie tried to scoot back but was stopped when her shoulders bumped against the wall. "Are you going to give me some space or are you going to force me to lay here while you finish?"

Clint stepped back slowly. "So long as you behave, we can both make ourselves a little more presentable."

"And after that?"

"After that, we talk."

Janie nodded. "Fine."

True to his word, Clint stepped back a little more until he was just out of her kicking range. He kept his eyes on her as he pulled his jeans back up and she got her skirt situated properly. When Clint bent down to pick up his gun belt, he saw Janie start to move like a bird that had been flushed from its hiding spot.

Clint was just fast enough to reach out and grab her arm before she could pluck the Colt from its holster. This time, he tossed her back with more force. Most of that force was still absorbed by the hay bale when Janie landed with a thump on her backside.

"Damn," Clint said. "That was impressive. I'll bet that kind of speed has gotten you out of plenty of bad spots."

Janie didn't say anything. Instead, she just locked her eyes on him with a venomous glare.

Clint kept one hand on his gun and flipped Janie's knife in the other. "So," he said, "how long have you been working with this killer?"

Janie didn't flinch. She blinked a few times, but it seemed forced and put on for Clint's benefit. "What killer?"

"The one who lit that fire."

She laughed once and started to get up. Stopping when she saw the warning look on Clint's face, she shook her head and said, "I don't know what the hell you're talking about."

"You're working with him," Clint stated. "I know it, so there's no reason to hide it."

"You don't know anything."

Nodding as he settled himself against a wall, Clint said, "All right, then. I'll tell you what I do know. First of all, you knew my name when I didn't ever introduce myself properly."

"You did when we first met. You just don't recall because of everything else that was happening."

"Fine. Second, you're still alive."

"And you're holding that against me?" she scoffed.

"After what I've seen of that killer, you're damn right I am.

I've tangled with that animal more than once and I can tell you he's not the sort who takes prisoners. He doesn't need to."

"I walked by and saw what he was doing," she explained. "That's why he grabbed me."

"He wanted folks to see that fire, and you weren't enough to keep him from lighting it. I wasn't even enough to stop him from doing that much. That man fears nothing, and he surely isn't the sort to hide behind an innocent woman. Besides, he only grabbed you after I showed up. What were you doing before then?"

Janie shook her head. "You're crazy. To think I would ever want to touch you."

"What did you say he said to you?" Clint asked.

"That he wanted to see me burn."

"Then why didn't he knock you out and throw you onto the pool of kerosene he'd just made?"

"You'll have to ask him that," Janie replied.

"I will. But first, I'd like you to tell me where I can find him."

She shook her head again and muttered, "You truly are crazy."

"Then why don't you just go home?" Snapping his fingers, Clint added, "That's right. Because you don't live here."

"And whatever made you come up with that?"

"I followed you after we parted ways the first time."

Janie blinked and did a good job of looking confused, but she wasn't quite good enough to hide the mix of surprise and panic in her eyes.

"And before you spout off some more lies," Clint said, "I'll have you know I saw you go to that house on the other end of town."

"And how do you know it wasn't mine?"

"I didn't. At least, not right away. I was a bit suspicious after I saw how the killer treated you, so I followed you. It seemed odd that you would lead me in one direction and then go in another, but I figured you might just be cautious. Then, I saw the killer standing at one of the windows looking outside like he was wishing upon a star. After all the hiding you two must have done, I would have thought he'd know enough to stay out of sight."

Janie shook her head, but couldn't think of what to say. Her eyes darted to the gun at Clint's side and then fixed upon the knife in his hand.

"You want this blade so bad you can taste it," Clint said. "Not exactly fitting for an innocent woman, now is it?"

"Go to hell," Janie hissed.

Now Clint shook his head. It was the only part of him that moved. Just as she was starting to look away from him, he lunged forward to grab her chin in one hand and hold her knife to her throat with the other.

"What are you . . . ?" she shouted.

Clint's eyes were narrowed to fiery slits. All he needed to do was cock his head a bit to let her know that she needed to quiet down.

In a whisper, she asked, "What are you doing?"

"You're a good liar," Clint said. "You're also not a bad fighter. Those kinds of talents don't just sprout up from nowhere." He pressed the blade to her neck at an angle that put more of the flat portion of it against her skin, but stared at her as if he was about to open her throat. "And this knife isn't the sort of thing someone carries around in case of emergencies."

"You won't kill me," she whispered.

"I saw you with him," Clint said. "I couldn't hear what you were saying, but you two were friendly enough. We're looking for more than one killer, and you may just be the other one we're after. That means you're already dead. After all those deaths in all those fires, you'll hang for sure."

Janie sneered at him as if she was about to spit. "Then why should I say anything to you?"

"Because you'll pray to take your chances with a judge the moment I get started in on you if you don't start telling me everything I need to know about who you are and who that big fellow is."

Janie glared defiantly at Clint, but couldn't find the first hint that he was lying. In fact, the longer she stared at him, the more she wanted to look away. Finally, she did look away.

"My real name is Elizabeth," she said and sighed.

Clint nodded and eased up on the blade a bit. "That's a good start."

THIRTY-SEVEN

There was a knock on Bower's door.

The Texas Ranger was slow to answer it, but he eventually opened the door just enough for him to look outside. Seeing the man standing there, he let out a tired sigh. "I just got through watching that street, Adams. Can't you let me get some sleep?"

"I've got a present for you," Clint said with a smile.

The statement was just odd enough to make Bower think he might be dreaming. "What did you say?"

Clint stepped aside a bit, allowing Bower to see that he was dragging something along with him. Actually, he was dragging someone, and that someone wasn't very happy. Elizabeth's arms were tied behind her back by shreds of velvet. Her dress was also missing several inches off the bottom of the skirt.

"This little lady is one of the killers you've been chasing," Clint said.

Bower pulled his door open and stepped aside so Clint could enter. "She's the one that was being held prisoner, isn't she?"

"Yes," Elizabeth said with half of a sob in her voice. "And I'm still a prisoner. Please—"

"She's also the one who tried to kill me," Clint cut in as he held out the knife he'd taken from her. "With this."

Bower shut the door and stared at the knife. He stared at her and then made a decision. "So she's the one, huh?"

"You're going to believe this crazy man?" Elizabeth asked.

"Sure. I never really could figure why that big fellow would start grabbing up prisoners anyway."

"Thank you," Clint said.

Elizabeth was pushed over to a chair in the corner of the room. Before her backside even hit the seat, she was snarling at Bower. "Go to hell, the both of you! I hope Lester keeps you alive and healthy until you start to burn!"

"Lester?" Bower asked.

Clint nodded. "Lester Voorhees. That's the man we're looking for. The big fellow."

"She told you that?"

"Yep. She was a bit more cooperative a little while ago."

"You mean while you were torturing me," Elizabeth said. "And raping me!"

Scowling down at her, Bower took a closer look. He even reached down to move her head from side to side. "You don't look tortured to me," he said finally.

"It's my word against his," she snapped while glaring at Clint.

When Bower looked at him, Clint said, "Some of her words from earlier had something to do with what she and Voorhees had planned next. She's also the one who led me to where Voorhees was staying here in town."

"Really?" Bower said. "Then what the hell are we doing here?"

"We're dropping her off here and then getting Mark back to keep an eye on her. Someone needs to watch her, and it might as well be him since he's still a bit hurt and probably tired after watching that street."

"You're still hurt and moving along just fine," Bower pointed out.

"Yeah, but I've had some rest. There's only three of us, so we need to be smart about who does what. Any little thing could make a big difference."

Bower started to nod. "You're right. I'll go get Mark." With that, the Texas Ranger bolted from the room.

Before the door stopped rattling from being slammed, Elizabeth was spitting at Clint. "He'll kill you, you know," she said. "He'll kill all of you."

Clint was at the bed, stripping it of all its sheets. "Is that a fact?"

"Yes, it is. The only bad thing is that I wish I could do it myself. If I ask real nice, Lester will save one for me. I'll make sure it's you."

Ripping up some sheets, Clint said, "Great. You do that."

"You'll never catch him. Not if you don't know where to look."

"I do know where to look," Clint told her. "Thanks to you."

"Oh, that's right. You and those lawmen are so good at tracking." She bit her lower lip and giggled. "If that was true, Lester and I wouldn't have gone for so long doing whatever the hell we want to do."

Clint walked up to her chair and started wrapping her up in the ripped sheets. Even when he thought he'd tied her up plenty tight enough, he kept wrapping some more just to be sure. "You hear those footsteps? That'd be the other two returning. From here, we go to catch your friend Lester and then this whole ride of yours is over."

"Just go catch him, huh?" Elizabeth shrugged and settled into her bonds. "Great. You do that."

THIRTY-EIGHT

Mark wasn't happy about staying behind to watch Elizabeth, but he didn't waste time putting up a fight. He followed Clint's instructions by keeping his gun on her no matter how tightly she was tied up. Just for safe measure, Clint had stuffed another bundle of ripped sheets in her mouth to keep her quiet.

Clint and Bower cut through every alley they could to get to the house across town. Once it was in sight, they slowed down and found a dark corner where they could get a look at the place before going in. There was no light coming from any window and no hint of any movement from inside.

"You sure this is the place?" Bower asked.

"Yep."

"And you're sure he's in there?"

Although he wished he could answer differently, Clint shook his head and said, "Nope."

"Fair enough. Let's get on with this, then."

Bower drew his pistol and ran toward the side of the house. Clint kept his hand on his Colt, but kept the gun holstered as he circled around the back of the house to approach the other side.

Along the way, he looked into the windows and searched for any trace of where Voorhees could be. Even the window through which he'd spotted Voorhees and Elizabeth was now dark. The place was also quiet. In fact, it was so quiet that it seemed unnatural.

Both men followed through on the plan they'd cobbled together while they'd been running across town. After circling the house, Clint made his way to the back door while Bower went to the front. Bower waited for the count of five before knocking on the door and then kicking it in. Rather than charge into the house, Bower jumped back and listened for any movement inside.

At the back of the house, Clint kept quiet and waited to see if Voorhees would come running out. Although he knew the man was fast, Clint also knew Voorhees was way too big to be able to run much of anywhere in that house without making a sound.

Swearing under his breath, Clint stepped up to the back door and found it to be ajar. He walked into the house and stepped carefully as his eyes acclimated to the thick shadows.

"Come on in, Bower," Clint shouted.

His voice echoed through the small house. Clint listened and searched every corner he could see for a sign of movement. Every shadow big enough to hide Voorhees was double-checked. Even after Bower came into the house, Clint didn't put down his guard.

"I smell something bad," Bower said.

Clint kept his eyes moving and replied, "I know. Me, too. I think it's coming from the bedroom. I'll head there and you watch my back."

Both men moved down the short hallway that led to the house's only other three rooms. As they came to a door, Clint kicked it in. For the most part, the rooms were small and sparsely furnished enough to be examined without stepping inside. The last door led to the room that Clint had peeked into before. Even before he opened that door, Clint could tell this was the room he wanted.

"Jesus, that's rank," Bower muttered.

They stepped inside to find the window open and a breeze

blowing the curtains about. On the bed and next to it were the corpses of the family who'd lived there.

"Aw, God," Bower said.

But Clint's eyes were more focused on the window. "Just check this room and be quick about it," he ordered. "Check every inch of it and then go through this house one more time."

Bower carried out Clint's orders to the letter. Within a minute or so, he returned to the bedroom shaking his head. "It's empty."

When Clint heard those words, he wasn't surprised. His next thought weighed on him even heavier than the sight of the dead family. "That window wasn't open when I came around this side of the house," Clint said.

"Are you sure?"

"Yeah. It was closed, which means he was just here."

Bower turned and slammed a frustrated fist against the wall. "God damn it all! You should have said that before, Adams! Let's get after him!"

"Too late," Clint said. "He moves too fast. We'd just be running around town like fools hoping to stumble on something."

"Isn't that what we are right now?"

Clint lowered his head. At that moment, he wasn't able to refute what Bower was saying.

The Texas Ranger jumped on that like a hungry coyote pouncing on a lame deer. "If he kills anyone else, it's on your head!"

"And what if he was just hiding here after opening that window to make us run out there after him?" Clint asked viciously. "It was a fifty-fifty shot that he did that as opposed to climbing out the window. Anyone who chases after men like this should know that!"

"We could have split up to—"

"Mark and I both tried taking him on alone and nearly got torn apart! You think you could've done better? I made a wrong choice, god damn it, don't tell me you've never done the same!"

Bower still looked ready to fight, but that faded quickly enough. Eventually, he nodded and said, "Every last one of us from Henry on down has let this bastard slip past us some way or another."

Reining himself in as well, Clint patted the Texas Ranger on the shoulder. "That ends now, because we've got an edge you've never had before."

"We sure do," Bower replied. "Mark's sitting with her right now."

THIRTY-NINE

Bower threw open the hotel room's door and stomped inside so quickly that he nearly caused Mark to fire on him. Mark had his gun drawn and was facing the door as if he was still deciding whether or not he should pull his trigger,

"Damn it, Bower," Mark snapped. "All you had to do was knock."

Ignoring his partner, Bower asked, "Where'd he go?"

Elizabeth shrugged as best she could considering she was still tied to her chair. Even after Clint pulled the gag from her mouth, she didn't make a sound.

"I won't ask you again," Bower said. "You tell us where to find him."

"I certainly have no idea what you're talking about," she replied.

Clint stepped around behind her so he could lean down close to her ear. "What she means is that she doesn't think she has a reason to help us. Maybe," he added while nodding to the other two behind Elizabeth's back, "we should tell her about the deal."

The Texas Rangers played along perfectly. Neither one of them seemed too confused and simply stared intently back at Clint. Finally, Bower spoke up.

"Go on," he said. "Tell her."

After what seemed like too much time had passed, Elizabeth tried to look over her shoulder. "What deal?" she asked,

"The one that'll save your life," Clint told her as he stepped around so she could look at his face. "Tell us where to find Voorhees and you'll just be known as an accomplice."

Even though she didn't say anything, Clint could practically hear what she was thinking. She was going through what she would say to a judge or jury, just as she'd planned out what she'd said to him when she'd first tried to convince Clint that she was Voorhees's prisoner.

More than likely, the two speeches were pretty much the same.

"Why would you offer this?" she asked.

Before Clint could say anything, Bower stepped up. "This is why," he said while showing her the badge.

Elizabeth looked at the badge and then started to laugh. "Texas Rangers? How long is your leash supposed to be?"

"Not long enough," Bower told her. "We can't come all this way and go home empty-handed. Bringing back a monster like Voorhees would do plenty to make all of this worth our while."

"And get you out of some hot water, I'll bet," she added.

Reluctantly, Bower nodded. It helped that he wasn't exactly lying in that regard.

"And if we can't get him," Clint whispered to her, "we've got you. You're not quite the same sort of animal as Voorhees, but you'll be a good enough offering to serve our purposes."

It didn't take long for Elizabeth to put together the bits and pieces she'd been given. Although he hadn't drawn her a complete picture, Clint figured she would come to the conclusion he'd been hoping for.

He was right.

Elizabeth's eyes lit up and she smiled broadly. "You don't have anything against me," she said. "There's no witnesses and no proof I did anything wrong. Just your word against mine."

While Clint had wanted her to get some confidence, he didn't want to make her feel too strong. He knocked her down a peg by saying, "Our word will be more than enough when we tell the same account after shooting you while you tried to escape."

Wincing at the sound of that, Elizabeth glanced at the faces of the two Texas Rangers. Neither Mark nor Bower gave her the slightest hope that they wouldn't follow through on Clint's threat. "Fine," she sighed. "What do you want me to do?"

"You're going to tell us where to find Voorhees," Bower said.

"And how do I know you'll keep your end of the deal?"

"You're just going to have to trust us."

Elizabeth laughed once under her breath. "I guess I don't have much choice."

Clint stepped around so he could look her in the eyes. "That's right. You don't."

"Loosen these sheets first," she grunted. "I can barely breathe."

Once that was done, Elizabeth bowed her head and said, "If we were split up, the plan was to head to Albuquerque and meet up there. Lester will keep quiet until we meet at a hotel there, but only for a few days. After that, he'll figure I'm dead or captured and will move on."

"Where will he go from there?" Bower asked.

"I don't know," she replied smugly. "So you boys had better get moving."

FORTY

Mark was able to contain himself for about five seconds after Clint led him out of the room. Halfway down the stairs, the Texas Ranger fumed. "This is horseshit! Are you and Bower actually believing a word that comes out of that bitch's mouth?"

Grabbing Mark's elbow so he could drag him outside, Clint told him, "We wouldn't believe her if she told us the sky was blue."

"Then why the hell are you dealing with her?"

"Because the only way she's of any use is if we let her do what she's good at and that's stabbing men in the back."

Mark winced as if the conflicting thoughts in his head were actually jamming him up inside. "So that house was empty?"

"Not quite. There were bodies in there that were killed with a knife. Since Voorhees has yet to swing a knife at anyone, I'd say she's the one who killed them."

"And now we're dealing with her? We're going all the way to Albuquerque on the word of a lying, murdering whore?"

"The only place we're going," Clint said calmly, "is to get our horses ready to ride. And we'd better be quick about it. Come on."

"So what the hell is going on here?"

Clint actually felt sorry for just how flustered Mark had gotten. "Come on. I'll talk as we get the horses."

The first rays of the sun were seeping into the sky, and the chill in the air acted like a splash of cold water in both men's faces. Apart from the few early risers and the marshal's deputy making his rounds, the streets were empty. When Clint spoke, he could do so in a whisper and still be heard just fine.

"You did a real good job when we were talking to her back there," Clint said. "I wish we'd had the time to tell you what we intended on doing earlier, but we'd just come up with it on our way back to the hotel."

"So you and Bower have a better plan than this?" Mark asked as he threw his saddle over his horse's back.

Clint was no stranger to saddling Eclipse in a hurry. He barely had to think about what he was doing as he went through motions that were practically second nature. "I hope it's better."

"Thank God. What is it?"

"We needed to convince her that she truly had to deal with us," Clint explained. "She needed to think she was still in trouble, but still have a slight glimmer of hope."

Cinching up the last buckle on his saddle, Mark grinned and said, "I'd say you did all those things pretty damn well. You sure had me fooled."

"Sorry about that. Like I said, that part was just out of necessity."

"Hey, no need for apologies. What's the next part of your plan?"

Climbing into his saddle and settling in, Clint replied, "We sit and wait for her to escape."

Mark had one foot in the stirrup and both hands on the saddle horn. Stopping just before pulling himself up, he stared at Clint and waited. When no more was forthcoming, he said, "What?"

"It's risky, but we don't have a lot of time. Voorhees is out of sight and could be anywhere by now. The best way for us to find him is to have someone take us straight to him, and I don't think that woman was going to do that anytime soon."

"Yeah, but . . . let her escape?"

Clint laughed and said, "That part wasn't my idea. It was Bower's, and I couldn't think of anything else to get results any faster."

"What if she hurts him?" Mark asked. "What if she kills him?"

"First of all, she's only escaping because we're going to let her escape. Second, since she thinks she's already put us on the wrong track, she'll rush to Voorhees as soon as she can. She won't have the time to hurt anyone."

"Are you sure about that?"

"Nope, but not much on this earth is for certain. Besides, we're not going to let her out of our sight for very long."

Mark groused. "I still don't like this. Besides, there's no way we know when she'll even try to . . ."

Mark's voice trailed off, and his eyes locked on something in the distance. When Clint turned to get a look at what he'd spotted, he grinned victoriously.

"And there he is now," Clint said.

Bower ran toward the stable with his hat in one hand while using his other hand to rub his head. Once he got closer, the blood on his hand could be seen. Despite that, he was still grinning from ear to ear.

"What happened to you?" Mark asked.

Ignoring the question, Bower slapped his hat back on and asked, "Is my horse ready?"

"Right over there," Clint replied.

The Texas Ranger jumped onto his horse's back and motioned for them to head out to the street and to the right. "We'll circle around the hotel," Bower whispered. "We should be able to catch up to her before long."

"What the hell happened?" Mark asked.

Bower looked at the other two men and then settled on Clint. "Didn't you tell him?"

"Sure he told me," Mark said. "But what he told me was crazy. You let her escape?"

Grinning and trying not to laugh, Bower said, "That arrogant bitch thought she was so slick wriggling out of those ropes, even though Clint needed to loosen them twice. I turned my back on her for a solid minute before she made her move and knocked me in the head with a lamp. Good thing it broke so easily, because she took off like a shot."

"And you don't think she'll be riding out of town right this instant?" Mark asked.

"Of course she will," Bower told him. "I already followed her a ways after she ran from the hotel. She must have really thought she knocked me out cold, because she stole a horse right from the corner and headed north."

"That'd take her back to Kipperway," Clint said.

Bower nodded and got his horse moving at a quick trot. "I know right where her trail starts, and it's early enough for it to still be there. We'll see which way she took to leave town, then track her to where she goes and scoop her up again when she gets there."

Although Mark was still fidgeting, he followed Bower and Clint back to the hotel. Bower hung off the side of his horse like an Indian riding bareback so he could get a better look at the street outside the Archer Hotel. "These tracks right here are hers. I got a real good look at those expensive boots she was wearing. This is where she stole the horse."

"And here's the freshest set of horse tracks," Clint said while pointing to the freshly trampled dirt.

Sure enough, there weren't any other horses in sight that could have left those tracks, and no other prints to mar the ones Clint had spotted.

"This could turn out to be a big mistake," Mark warned.

Bower shrugged and grinned. "At the least, all this running will tucker her out so she'll be easier to take back to Texas. At the most, we'll get to the other one."

Mark still looked as if he couldn't believe what was happening. "You really think this is a good idea?"

"Hell, this sort of thing is why I wanted to join the Rangers in the first place."

FORTY-ONE

When Clint walked back into the Kipperway Tavern later that afternoon, he found Henry sitting there as if he was holding court. In fact, it seemed as if Clint had never even left. It didn't take long for Henry to notice him and wave him over to his table.

"Good to see you, Adams," Henry said. "What's so damn funny?"

Clint wiped the grin off his face and took a seat next to the Texas Ranger. "Just that I've been gone for a while and you're in the same spot as when I left you."

"Yeah, well maybe sitting still ain't so bad. I heard there was some trouble over your way."

"You heard about that, huh?" Clint asked.

Henry nodded. "Solace ain't that far away, you know."

"Well, I haven't heard anything from here, so you must've been taking it easy."

The Texas Ranger let out a guffaw and leaned back to catch the bartender's eye. "You hear that? Clint thinks I've been sitting on my ass the whole time."

"That sure ain't so!" the bartender said. "You drink free here so long as I own this place."

"And that's better than the wages the town law gets paid around here," Henry told Clint with a wry grin.

"Was there any more trouble from Red or any of those others that tried to loot the Wilkins place?"

"I thought you'd never ask," Henry said proudly. "They tried to make a move on me and Talman just as soon as you left."

Clint glanced around, but saw no trace of Talman.

"And before you get yer hopes too high," Henry said, "we rounded them up without taking more than a scratch or two ourselves."

"Talman and I may not have seen eye to eye, but I wasn't hoping for the man to catch a bullet." Upon seeing the stern scowl on the older man's face, Clint shrugged. "Well, maybe it would've been acceptable if he got a flesh wound."

"Mean, but honest. I like that. What about you, Adams? Have any luck over in Solace?"

Now it was Clint's turn to strut. "While you and Talman were hooking your bunch of local minnows, Bower, Mark and I were catching the big fish."

Henry leaned forward and grabbed hold of the table. "You caught him?"

"We locked horns with him, but we caught her."

"Her?"

Clint told the Texas Ranger what had happened while he was gone and helped himself to a beer along the way. Since he gave the shortened account, Clint's mug wasn't even half-empty by the time he was done.

Letting out a breath, Henry leaned back in his chair as if he'd been dropped into it. "You . . . let . . . her . . . go?"

Clint nodded. "It's all a part of a plan so we could—"

"You let her go? What in the hell were you hoping to accomplish by that? Do you know how long we've been tracking them down?"

"Yeah," Clint replied sternly. "And in all that time you didn't even know one of the people you were after was a woman."

"We had our suspicions."

"Well, if you don't want to hear the best part of this whole thing, I can let you scream while I finish my beer."

"Fine," Henry grunted. "What's the best part?"

"The best part is that the plan worked."

Some of the anger in Henry's eyes faded when he heard that. "Really?"

"Do you think I'd be sitting here enjoying a beer if it hadn't?"

"I suppose not. How well did it work?"

"Well enough that we found where they are."

"Both of them?" Henry asked hopefully.

Clint nodded. "Both of them. Mark and Bower are keeping an eye on them as we speak. They're supposed to come get us if either of those killers makes a move to leave town, and I wouldn't count on them sitting still for too long."

Henry jumped from his chair and marched toward the door. "Take me to those sons of bitches. I've got something I've been meaning to tell them."

FORTY-TWO

Clint took Henry to a small dry goods store on the north end of town. Giving a nod to the little old man behind the counter, Clint led the Ranger straight to the back of the store and into a small supply room. Mark and Bower were already there. To Clint's surprise, Talman, Barkley and Dave had joined them as well.

"Look who we found while you were away," Bower said as he pointed toward the other three Rangers.

Barkley extended a paw of a hand toward Clint, which was immediately shaken. "Glad to see you're still with us, Adams," the tracker said. "I heard there was some trouble in Solace."

Clint looked over to Henry, only to see the older man shrug.

"Barkley keeps his ear to the ground better than anyone," Henry said. "That's why we keep him."

Although Clint acknowledged Talman's presence with a friendly nod, he only got half a grin in return before the Ranger spat a wad of dark juice onto the floor.

Stepping over to the only window in the room, Clint looked out through the small square opening and across the street. "What have they been doing all this time?"

That question put a smirk on all of the Rangers' faces except for Henry. Clint settled upon Mark and stared the Ranger down until he got his answer.

"We're not certain," Mark muttered, "but it seems they've been, ahhh, making up for lost time."

"What?"

"Near as we can tell . . . they've . . ."

Barkley cut in. "They've been humping like dogs in mating season. I could hear her hollering enough to be certain."

Shaking his head, Henry stepped up to the window to get a look for himself. Apart from the little house at the corner, there wasn't much else to see. "They're bold, I'll give 'em that much. I want someone to get up there and take a closer look."

Talman started to step forward, but he was cut off before he could throw his hat into the ring.

"What I meant was, I want Barkley to take a closer look," Henry added. "He's the only one who can get up there and back without being spotted."

Barkley tipped his hat and walked toward the door. He was gone before Talman had enough time to start complaining.

Clint ignored Talman's grousing so he could focus on what was happening outside. With just a little bit of concentration, he could hear the faint sound of a woman's moan.

"She's a loud one, all right," Dave said.

Glancing quickly at the young Ranger, Clint said, "You've been picking up a lot of Barkley's habits. I didn't even realize you were there."

"He's teaching me to be a real tracker."

"Well, he's a good one to learn from in that regard. Take a look for yourself."

Dave looked through the window for a few seconds before spotting Barkley making his way from one spot to another as he closed in on the small house. Even though he knew Barkley was out there, as well as where the tracker was headed, Clint lost sight of the man every so often.

"There wasn't anyone in that house before, was there?" Clint asked.

Talman shook his head and spat a wad of tobacco so it landed within inches of Clint's boot. "Nah. I scouted it out myself. And if you don't believe me, you can take Barkley's word for it when he gets back."

"I believe you," Clint replied. "You've got to be good for something."

Everyone but Talman got a chuckle out of that. Although Clint hadn't looked away from the window for more than a second or two, Barkley was already on his way back to the store when he looked out again.

The tracker moved swiftly across the street and quickly made his way to the back room where the rest of the Rangers were waiting. "They're still in there," he said. "At least, the big fellow still is."

"What about the woman?" Henry asked.

Barkley shrugged. "I didn't see her, but I couldn't see every corner inside that house."

Henry checked his pistol to make sure it was fully loaded. "We're going right now. Barkley, you and Dave circle around back of that house. Mark and Bower, you two fan out along the street to see if you can spot the woman. Talman and Clint, we're going straight ahead."

Everyone nodded and checked his gun. Not another word was said as all the men followed Henry's lead and filed out of the store.

FORTY-THREE

Clint, Henry and Talman were first out of the store and stepped immediately into the street so they could approach the house head-on. Dave and Barkley came out next and moved ahead quickly to disappear into the alleys so they could make their approach around back of the house. As ordered, the remaining two men fanned out and kept their eyes on everything else other than the house.

As Clint got closer to the house, he felt as if the place was getting smaller and smaller. It was two floors high, but only slightly wider than a single room. By the looks of the place, it could have been part of the neighboring structure at one time or another. Putting those stray thoughts aside, Clint focused on the task at hand. From what he'd already seen of the two they were after, he was going to need to be extra sharp if they were going to be brought down without any more casualties.

Henry climbed the single step that led from the street to the house's front door, but paused before making another move. Once he saw Clint and Talman take positions on either side of him, he reached out and knocked.

"Come on out, Voorhees," Henry announced. "This is the only chance you're getting, so make the best of it. If we have to come in after you, it's gonna get ugly."

All three men outside that door were like coiled springs.

They stood ready to fight as their senses strained for any trace of movement on the other side of that door.

Clint was standing to Henry's left. Although there was no window there, he could hear the subtle scratch of something moving against a dirty floor. Along with that, Clint heard two clicks that sent a chill down his spine.

Reaching out to grab Henry's collar, Clint pulled the Ranger away from the door just as a shotgun nearly cut the door in half.

The shotgun blast was deafening from that distance. Splinters of wood filled the air, and smoke poured through the gaping hole in the door. Clint still had Henry by the collar and had to look at the Ranger carefully to make certain he'd acted quickly enough. Judging by the stunned look on Henry's face, even he wasn't sure whether or not he'd survived intact.

Finally, Henry nodded and said, "I'm all right."

As soon as he heard that, Talman flipped his gun to his left hand and then drew the second gun from his double-rig holster. He stretched out his left arm and fired a shot into the house before stepping up to the doorway and unleashing both of his barrels.

"Talman is good for something, you know," Henry said.

Clint chuckled under his breath and drew his Colt so he could join Talman. The other Ranger was already inside, pulling his triggers and filling the entire house with the roar of gunfire.

Rather than join Talman in making holes in the walls, Clint squinted through the smoke to find a target. The inside of the house seemed even smaller than the outside. There was no furniture to be seen, which told Clint that the reports of the place being empty could be trusted. Even so, the place was still a bit emptier than he would have liked.

"Keep going toward the back and flush him out," Clint said once Talman paused to reload.

Talman sent the spent casings to the floor and reloaded in a series of quick, practiced movements. In no time at all, he was snapping his guns shut and looking for something to shoot. "What about you?" he asked.

Clint pointed to the narrow, broken staircase to his right without saying a word. Nodding, Talman continued his walk through the house.

The stairs were noisy and felt as if they were one stiff breeze from falling over. Clint kept to the side of each stair and knew he was on the right track when he saw another set of fresh footprints in the dust.

Knowing better than to charge straight up the stairs, Clint went as quickly as he could without taking too much of a risk. As it turned out, his caution almost wasn't enough to keep his head on his shoulders.

The only thing at the top of the stairs was a pair of large boots. As soon as Clint saw them, he dropped down and pressed his chest against the top stair. Voorhees pulled one of his shotgun's triggers and emptied its barrel into the wall a foot or two over Clint's head.

Clint had wound up a little closer to Voorhees than he'd hoped, but that distance kept him just outside of the spread of buckshot coming from the shotgun's barrel. He didn't waste any time counting his blessings before climbing the rest of the stairs and pulling his own trigger.

Voorhees backed into the room as smoke curled from the end of his shotgun. Even though he tracked Clint with the weapon, he was reluctant to pull his trigger.

Clint was reluctant to fire as well. "What's the matter, Voorhees?" Clint asked. "Afraid of setting off that kerosene? I thought you'd be drinking the stuff by now."

Voorhees grinned, but didn't take his eyes off Clint to glance at the containers of kerosene stacked against the wall. Still grinning, the big man turned at the waist to take aim at the containers.

Clint was still hoping to keep the kerosene from being sparked, which was why he hesitated to pull his trigger.

Voorhees, on the other hand, didn't have any such reservations. When he fired the second barrel of his shotgun, he did it without hesitation. The sparks from the barrel alone were almost enough to get the fire going. Once the buckshot ripped through the metal containers, the kerosene within ignited with a loud rush of heat.

"Too late to stop me now," Voorhees said as Clint watched in shock as the fire spread to consume the room. "This place is just the fuse! You and everyone else in this town are dead!"

FORTY-FOUR

When Clint and Talman were heading into the house, Barkley had caught sight of a slender figure running along the backs of the neighboring buildings. The figure was moving quickly, but Barkley could still see well enough to know that it was the woman he'd seen before.

The next thing Barkley did was look for his young apprentice. Just when he'd thought Dave wasn't around, he saw the Texas Ranger leap out from another alley and land in front of Elizabeth. Barkley ran as quickly as he could, as gunshots erupted from the house behind him. As much as he wanted to turn around and see what he could do to help Clint, Henry and the others, he knew his job was to nab that woman.

Dave had managed to wrap his arms around her, but Elizabeth was fighting back with everything she had. She dropped what looked like a waterskin as she was lifted off her feet by Dave. Kicking and screaming like a crazed woman, Elizabeth hit Dave anywhere she could as Barkley rushed in to help out.

A split second before Barkley closed the distance between them, Elizabeth got free of Dave's grasp and whipped around to face him. Her boots had barely touched the ground before she snapped out one arm and made a quick slash at Dave's neck. There was a glint of steel in Elizabeth's hand as Dave let out a surprised yelp and staggered back.

When she turned around to face Barkley again, the Texas Ranger was already bearing down on her.

He reached out to grab Elizabeth, but pulled his arms back when he saw her take a swing at him with her knife. The thin blade sliced through the air twice, each time coming close enough for Barkley to feel the breeze caused by her passing arm.

Barkley tried to get ahold of her again, but only snagged a bit of her sleeve before she tried to slash at him again. This time, Elizabeth was too close to get a proper swing at Barkley and her arm bounced off the man's wrist.

Lifting her off her feet with ease, Barkley tossed Elizabeth against a wall and then locked a solid grip around her wrist just above the knife in her grasp. Barkley gritted his teeth with the effort of holding her in place. Although she wasn't stronger than him, Elizabeth had more than enough steam in her to give him a run for his money.

She kicked and thrashed against him, just as she had with Dave. With her knife arm being held in place, she'd lost the edge that had allowed her to escape the first time.

Barkley took her wrist and slammed it against the wall. "Drop it!" he snarled.

Her fingers tightened around the knife's handle, and she snapped her head forward as if she meant to bite him.

"I said drop it!" With that, Barkley slammed her hand back again. This time, he got her to loosen her grip on the knife and let it drop to the ground. Barkley immediately stepped on the knife to keep it under his boot.

"Real big man," Elizabeth said through gritted teeth. "Harming a woman rather than test your strength against Lester."

Despite the fact that he knew just how dangerous this woman was, Barkley wasn't able to get past what she was saying. It became clear that those same words were echoing inside of him as he seemed to be frozen in his spot.

Elizabeth winced and started to heave against Barkley's

strong hands. There were no tears coming down her face, but she was doing enough acting to make it seem otherwise.

"Where are you, Dave?" Barkley asked. When he turned to get a look at where the younger Ranger had landed, Barkley felt Elizabeth's boot pound against his groin.

Barkley let out a pained wheeze as his grip loosened just a little. That little bit was all Elizabeth needed to tear herself free. Before she could take one more step, she saw Dave reach for her and grab her by the throat.

Although Dave didn't choke her, he balled up a fist and used it to flatten her nose against her face. Elizabeth's head knocked against the wall and she dropped to the ground in an unconscious heap.

"God damn," Barkley said as he struggled to stand up straight.

Dave offered his hand to Barkley and shrugged. "Call me whatever you like, but that bitch tried to kill me. I owed her at least that much."

Looking over to his partner, Barkley was glad to see a long cut going across the top of Dave's chest. The cut was bleeding, but it seemed shallow and was a few inches south of his jugular. "I won't call you anything," he grunted. "I just wished I could've been the one to put her down. What's that?"

Following Barkley's line of sight, Dave found the water-skin Elizabeth had dropped. He picked it up and held it to his nose. "Kerosene," he said.

Just then, both men noticed the smoke coming from the second floor of the house, where Voorhees had been hiding.

"Aw, Jesus," Barkley said. "Even if we did stop her from pouring that shit along here, this whole street could still go up."

"You go help the others," Dave said. "I'll gather some folks to help put this fire out before it spreads."

Barkley took the knife from Elizabeth's hand and picked her up. She wasn't a big woman, but she was still dead weight and his legs were still a bit wobbly. Before too long, he had her slung over his shoulder and was walking toward the smoking building.

He could hear gunshots coming from that direction, as well as several people shouting from the building as well as the street.

An inferno was sinking its teeth into the town of Kipperway. Barkley prayed something could be done before every dusty building was brought down in the wildfire.

FORTY-FIVE

Clint raised his Colt to fire a shot, but had to duck as Voorhees swung the empty shotgun at him like a club. Before Clint could take another opportunity to fire, the shotgun was being swung straight down at him like a sledgehammer. Clint rolled to one side, turned and fired at the spot where Voorhees had been.

The only problem was that Voorhees was no longer there. Instead, the big man had dashed around to Clint's left and was close enough to bring the shotgun down in a quick chopping motion that caught Clint on the right forearm.

Although no bones were broken, Clint reflexively let go of the Colt. In the next instant, he reached down for it with his left hand. Voorhees was already swinging at the gun and managed to swat it away by using the shotgun.

When Voorhees turned to show Clint a victorious smile, he caught Clint's fist dead in the mouth. Voorhees was stunned by the quick punch and blinked to try to clear his vision. As he staggered toward one of the windows of the single upstairs room, Voorhees heard a voice from the street below.

"Right there, Mark!" Henry shouted. "Left window!"

The glass in the window shattered as gunfire blazed up from the street.

Voorhees instinctually moved away from the window and stepped directly in front of Clint. Clasping his hands together, Clint swung both arms up to catch Voorhees in the chin. The big man stumbled, and let out a pained yell when Clint brought both elbows straight down to slam into Voorhees's arm.

This time, Voorhees was the one who lost his weapon, as the pain from Clint's blow forced him to let go of the shotgun. Voorhees stumbled away from Clint while wildly swatting at him with both hands.

"He's at your window now, Henry!" another of the Rangers shouted from outside.

More gunshots from street level tore through the window directly behind Voorhees. A few rounds clipped the big man, adding more wounds to the ones he'd gotten near the other window.

Clint wanted to grab his Colt with the time the others had bought him, but he saw that the pistol had come to rest just inside a patch of roaring flames against the wall.

"You're dead!" Voorhees said as the fire swelled within the small room. "Even if I die, I'm taking you with me!"

Stomping toward Clint like an enraged bull, Voorhees reached out for him with both hands. Suddenly a few gunshots punched up through the floor and tore into the big man's leg while also punching a hole through his foot. Even with those wounds, Voorhees made sure to throw himself forward to get ahold of Clint.

Dropping down at the last moment, Clint avoided Voorhees and grabbed the only weapon he could reach. The shotgun may have been empty, but it had already proven to be a good club. Clint jumped to his feet and swung the shotgun so its stock caught Voorhees in the small of his back.

The big man staggered forward a few more steps and let out a yelp as his hands and arms were forced into the fire. He tried to turn away from the blaze, but caught another blow in the shoulder.

Clint swung the shotgun so hard that he felt the strain in both shoulders. It bounced off Voorhees's muscled torso, as well as some of the flesh wounds the Rangers outside had given him. Voorhees made one last lunge toward Clint, but landed on the foot that had just been shot.

Seeing the big man stumble and lose his balance, Clint extended both arms to stab the shotgun directly into Voorhees's stomach. It took another push, but Clint finally shoved the big man into the fire that had grown to consume half of the room.

Voorhees screamed and flailed as the fire enveloped him. Soon, his screams died away and his melting body thumped to the floor.

Since the entire building was creaking and filling with smoke, Clint made one last dash across the room to a spot close to the top of the stairs. He bent at the knees and swept the shotgun against the floor to knock his Colt out of the flames. The pistol was charred, but not beyond repair. The iron burned his hands a bit, but hadn't been in the flames long enough to do any damage.

With the Colt wrapped in the bottom part of his jacket, Clint lowered his head and ran down the stairs before they collapsed. Talman was waiting there to guide him through the smoke and out the front door.

"I heard that bastard stomping around up there and thought I'd lend a hand," Talman said after getting outside. "Hope I came close to hitting him and not you."

Clint hacked up a few breaths and then filled his lungs with fresh air. There was a bucket brigade forming and they were waiting anxiously nearby.

"You did great," Clint said to Talman.

Talman nodded and turned his head so he could spit his tobacco without coming close to getting any on Clint's foot.

"Is that son of a bitch dead?" Henry asked.

"Yeah," Clint replied. "If that didn't kill him, nothing will."

"All right," Henry shouted to the bucket brigade. "Let's get to work!"

The fire didn't look so bad from outside. Clint caught his breath and then joined in with dousing the flames before they spread. Even after the fire was out, he found himself standing in the street to wait for one last attack from Voorhees.

It didn't come.

"Great job, Adams," Henry said after the building was a

smoking shell. "You ever need anything next time you're in Texas, you let me know."

"Will do," Clint replied. "Now, you'd better get yourselves back in your own jurisdiction before there's hell to pay."

"What about you? We could use a man like you."

Clint looked across the street at the milling crowd and spotted Belle among the curious faces. He saw her smile at him, and he waved to her and said, "I think I'll stay here. I could use a bath."

Watch for

DYING WISH

314th novel in the exciting GUNSMITH series
from Jove

Coming in February!

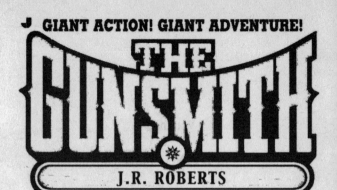